A FATE WORSE
THAN DEATH
& More Fright with a Bite

D0650766

Welcome to your worst nightmare

Arm in arm, Leslie and Marcia nervously wandered into the heart of Dracula's Castle. Their flashlight beams punched through the inky darkness, revealing room after room empty of anything but the dust and debris left from decades of neglect.

The girls turned to continue their search—only to find a man standing directly in front of them. Over six feet tall, he was completely bald and had gray, bloodless skin. His red, ratlike eyes glistened in the darkness, and when he smiled, he revealed two long, snakelike fangs.

"You have trespassed on cursed ground," the creature growled. "And now you are *mine!*"

The vampire's breath was strong and foul, like the smell of a rotting corpse. His entire body carried the stench of death.

Locking eyes with the vampire, Leslie and Marcia screamed with all the power in their lungs. Then they turned and bolted, racing headlong for the front door.

Leslie was the first to get there. She threw open the door, leaped off the porch, and stumbled down the broken walkway. Only then did she pause to look back for her friend.

"Marcia!" she called, turning back toward the evil old house. "Marcia! Where are you?"

But there was no reply. Marcia was nowhere to be seen.

A FATE WORSE THAN DEATH
& More Fright with a Bite

by Allen B. Ury

Troll

For Renee
—A.B.U.

Contents

Death on Colony Four

here is life on the moon. I know because I live there. Buried ten meters beneath the bleak lunar surface, my home is one of five miniature cities that have been built here over the last seventy-five years. Here, a quarter of a million miles from our Mother Planet, hundreds of men, women, and children representing over twenty different countries are currently working, playing, falling in love, going to school, and carrying on all the other day-to-day activities that make up human existence.

Of course, wherever life goes, death follows. And on the moon there are many ways to die—more, in fact, than people on Earth ever consider. Along with the usual reasons for dying—accidents, disease, and, of course, old age—lunar colonies offer such exotic exits as hypoxia (lack of oxygen), radiation poisoning, and flash freezing. My all-time favorite is depressurization, which happens when the air leaks out of a habitat or pressure suit, causing the gases in the victim's blood to boil and his or her organs to explode.

Those of us who live on the moon have come to accept death, even *bizarre* deaths, as a simple fact of, well, life. But every so often a pattern of unusual deaths makes the Lunar Project commanders sit up and take notice. Such as when a new virus appears and the victims have to be quarantined so the disease doesn't devastate our habitat. Or when long-term lunar residents suffer violent "Moon Madness," a mental illness believed to be caused by a combination of claustrophobia and prolonged isolation. Or when a vampire shows up and drains the life out of four people.

I heard about the first vampire death from my friend Elena Muravina. I was walking out of physics class when she told me. It was 1500 hours, which is three in the afternoon on Earth, and I was on my way home when Elena came running up behind me.

"Gretchen!" she said breathlessly in her slight Russian accent. "Did you hear about what happened last night in Sci-Lab B?"

Elena's father is our colony's Chief of Security, so she always has the inside track on unusual goings-on.

"No," I said eagerly. "Tell me."

"One of the new scientists, Dr. Kessler from Germany, was found dead in his bed," Elena said in a near whisper with all the secret glee of an old-time camp counselor telling ghost stories around a roaring campfire.

"What did he die from?" I asked, hoping for something *really* weird.

"I don't know. It's all a big mystery," Elena said,

grinning. "I asked my father, but he said it's a matter of top security."

I could hardly contain myself. "That must mean—"

"*Murder!*" Elena said, completing my thought.

"Were you able to find out anything?" I asked, pressing her for details.

"Well, I know that Dr. Kessler came up from Earth just a week ago, and that he was probably poisoned," Elena revealed.

"Poisoned?" I asked. "What makes you think that?"

"There were no signs of violence. No gunshot was heard, and no stab or laser wounds were found," Elena reported. "That leaves only poison."

"Wait a minute," I said, suddenly confused. "If there were no signs of violence, how do you know it *was* murder?"

"Because Commander McCormick has put my father in charge of the investigation," Elena said. "My father does not investigate deaths by natural causes."

Elena was right. If her father was investigating Dr. Kessler's death, then it had to be foul play. However, we heard nothing more about the case until four days later when another colonist, this time a maintenance engineer named Jonathan Banks, was found dead in one of the air shafts. Once again the details of the death were kept secret, although Elena managed to pick up a few choice details from her father at the dinner table.

"His death was like Dr. Kessler's—no signs of physical violence," Elena whispered to me as we sat in a corner of the colony's food court, underneath a strikingly realistic holographic image of the Rocky Mountains. "This time I managed to get a quick glimpse of an autopsy photo on my father's computer."

"And?" I asked eagerly, knowing my Russian friend was about to reveal something really juicy.

Elena pointed two fingers at the side of her neck. "Right here," she said. "There were two puncture wounds."

"You mean, like needle marks?" I asked with a slight shiver. I hated getting shots, and the thought of some mad killer running around injecting people gave me the creeps.

Elena shook her head. "No, they were too big for needles."

"What then?" I asked.

Elena took a moment to respond, as if she was afraid to say what she was thinking. "More like tooth marks," she finally admitted. "Fangs."

I thought about this for several seconds. My first thought was that the killer was using a poisonous snake to kill his or her victims. But poisonous animals of any kind weren't allowed on the moon, and anyone trying to sneak one in would have been caught by Security.

This was getting very interesting.

"All right, let's start with the basics," I said. "What did Dr. Kessler and Jonathan Banks have in common?"

"As far as I know, absolutely nothing," Elena said with a shrug. "Dr. Kessler was from Germany, had been here just a week, and was working on vaccines in the Bio-Med section. Mr. Banks was from Texas, in the United States, and had been here for three years. He was a Level Four maintenance engineer. He didn't even work near the Bio-Med section."

Once again Elena and I were at a loss for

explanations. And from what Elena told me, her father wasn't doing much better.

Three days later, a British astronomer named Laura Ashford was found dead, slumped over her computer console. Elena and I decided to take matters into our own hands.

After school we cornered Lee Tionawa, the smartest student in our computer class and perhaps the best cybernetics mind in the entire colony. We told him we wanted him to break into the colony's security files and find any information he could about the three mystery murders.

"Those are classified files," Lee noted.

"Exactly," Elena said. "They're double-coded, encrypted, and require two separate security clearances for access. Only a genius could crack them."

"Cool," Lee said, smiling.

Two hours later we were in Lee's bedroom gathered around his flat-screen computer monitor, watching excitedly as Dr. Kessler's autopsy report came into view.

"Fascinating," Lee said softly.

"What do you see?" I demanded impatiently.

"Apparently the cause of death was massive blood loss," Lee said, his eyes fixed on the glowing screen. "The only wounds on the body were two puncture marks on the right side of his neck."

"What about Banks and Ashford?" Elena asked. Lee clicked several icons and the next two autopsy reports joined Kessler's.

"The same," Lee said, arching his eyebrows. "Apparently Colony Four has become the hunting ground for some sort of . . ." He stopped short.

"Some sort of *what*?" I demanded.

"Vampire," Lee responded, sounding as if even he didn't believe what he was saying.

"But there are no vampires," Elena insisted. "They were proven to be nothing but the fantasies of a bunch of creative people back in the nineteenth and twentieth centuries."

"I know," Lee said, checking the reports again. "But *something* sucked the blood from these people. If it's not a real vampire, then it's someone who's *acting* like one."

I took a few moments to think about this. All I knew about vampires was what I'd read in books and seen in horror holo-tapes. I knew that vampires were supposed to be immortal and drank the blood of the living. Well, we had plenty of living people here on Colony Four to snack on. I also knew that vampires only came out at night because sunlight was deadly to them. Well, here, ten meters underground, there was no sunlight. This meant that a vampire—if there really was such a thing— could move about freely twenty-four hours a day.

Finally, I knew that the only way to kill a vampire— except for exposing it to sunlight—was to drive a wooden stake through its heart. On the Moon, we *had* no wood except for some souvenir pencils and a few decorative items. Everything, from the walls around us to the beds we slept in, was made from metal alloys or plastics. In other words, our lunar colony was the perfect hunting ground for this kind of killer.

"These murders started only ten days ago," Elena said, breaking my train of thought. "Who arrived from Earth in the past two weeks?"

Lee rapidly clicked a few more commands. A short list of names appeared on his monitor.

"Just four people have arrived in the past month," he reported. "One of them was Dr. Kessler."

"We can rule him out," I said dryly.

"The others were Ye Chung, a physicist from China; Abner Gordon, an engineer from the United States; and Lois Prescott, a doctor from Australia," Lee said, reading from the list.

"Too bad none of them is from Transylvania," Elena sighed. "That would certainly have narrowed things down."

A thought occurred to me. "Doctors deal with blood a lot," I said. "If I were a vampire, that's the kind of profession I'd choose. Is there a picture of Dr. Prescott in the files?"

Lee clicked on a few icons and a photo of an attractive, dark-haired woman appeared on the screen. She looked about thirty years old.

"She's cute," Lee commented.

"How old is she?" I continued.

Lee checked her history. His face registered concern. "According to this, she was born in 2081. That would make her—"

"At least fifty," said Elena, finishing his thought.

"She looks awfully good for fifty," I commented. Even with modern anti-aging treatments, it was still difficult for people to erase all the signs left by the passing years. "I'll bet a week's rations that she's our vampire."

"So what do we do about it?" Lee asked. He turned to Elena. "Do we tell your father?"

"He'll think we're crazy," Elena said. "Even if he

agrees with us, he can't risk his reputation by accusing someone of being a vampire."

"Then it's up to us," I said grimly. "We have to find a way to stop her. And fast."

I glanced at the calendar on Lee's wall. In addition to the usual Earth months, weeks, and days, moon calendars show lunar "days" and "nights," those prolonged periods when we either face the blazing sun or turn outward toward cold interstellar space. A new lunar day was due to start tomorrow.

"Lee, can you send Dr. Prescott e-mail?" I asked.

"Sure," Lee said. "That's easy."

"All right," I began. "Here's my plan."

* * *

Two days and one more mysterious murder later, Elena, Lee, and I were all standing in a corner of Landing Bay One, adjusting the fittings on our pressure suits. A circular landing pad protected by a retractable dome, the landing bay was one of the few areas of the colony actually located on the lunar surface.

"Are you reading me, Elena?" I asked.

"Loud and clear," Elena's Russian-accented voice echoed in my helmet.

"Lee?" I asked, turning toward the young computer whiz.

"Ten-four," he said, smiling at me through his helmet visor.

"I hope this works," Elena said with a sigh. "Or we are going to be in very big trouble."

"We'll be in trouble either way," I said curtly. "But if we're right, at least the killings will stop."

Just then, a tone sounded in my helmet.

"Someone's coming," Lee said. Together, we quickly moved behind one of the large cargo containers the recently departed Earth shuttle had left behind. In these crates were a variety of items needed for the colony's continued existence and growth: scientific equipment, food, clothing, entertainment programs . . . and medicine. Although we had no idea exactly *what* medicines were in this particular shipment, Lee had e-mailed Dr. Prescott with a message indicating they included blood products. We hoped that the mere thought of blood would be enough to lure the vampire—if, in fact, she was a vampire—into our trap.

So far our plan was working perfectly. On the other side of the enclosed landing bay, a pressure door hissed open. A woman I immediately recognized as Dr. Lois Prescott walked through. She looked around as if afraid of being spotted, then hurried across the bay toward the huge container behind which we were hiding.

Now came the hard part.

Reaching behind me, I hit the manual override controls that opened the bay's retractable dome. Instantly a siren sounded and yellow warning lights began to flash.

Startled, Dr. Prescott stood stone-still for several key seconds. Then, alarmed, she turned and raced back toward the pressure door.

Elena, Lee, and I sprang into action. Jumping out from behind the cargo containers, we bounded across the empty bay. Aided by the moon's weak one-sixth gravity, we threw ourselves at the fleeing physician, tackling her to the ground.

"What are you doing?" Prescott screamed, trying to kick us off her. "Let me go!"

Prescott was amazingly strong for such a small woman, and it took all three of us to hold her in place. Now the warning lights turned red, meaning the bay was about to depressurize. This was the moment of truth.

Above, the dome's six sections separated and began to retract like flower petals in reverse, revealing the black, star-filled sky above. Prescott let out an unearthly howl and threw Elena aside. Then, thrusting her elbow into my rib cage and momentarily winding me, she managed to get back to her feet.

Now I knew that Dr. Prescott had to be a vampire. Or at least she wasn't human. All lunar landing bays are equipped with a fail-safe abort system. If the bay's bio-sensor system had detected anyone in the bay not wearing a space suit, it would not have allowed the dome to retract. Since the dome was retracting, it meant that the sensors did not register Prescott as a human being.

With only Lee now clutching her leg, Prescott staggered over to the pressure door and hit the controls. But now that the bay was exposed to raw vacuum, the computers would not open the door because this would cause the colony's air supply to be sucked into space. She slammed her fist into the controls over and over again, but the door still refused to budge.

The instruments in my space suit helmet informed me that there was no longer any air left in the bay and that the temperature had plummeted to two hundred and fifty degrees below zero. Somehow Dr. Prescott, who was dressed only in her standard work clothes, was still alive and well.

Enraged, she turned to me and exposed two snake-like fangs. She snarled something at me, but it was impossible to hear her, since there was no air to carry sound waves. Then she lunged at me open-mouthed and prepared to sink her razor-sharp teeth into the neck of my space suit.

Had Prescott's fangs penetrated the thin mesh that separated my body from the cold vacuum of space, my suit would have depressurized within seconds and my blood gases would have exploded inside me. However, just at that moment the dome sections fully retracted. The first burst of unfiltered light blasted in from the blazing sun, now barely peaking over the horizon.

The light hit Dr. Prescott like a lightning bolt, blasting her clear across the bay and slamming her body up against the opposite wall. She hung there for a moment, pinned to the wall, her feet dangling a good three inches off the floor as her arms and legs violently thrashed about. Then steam began to rise from her body, turning to shimmering vapor in the sub-zero cold of space. As I looked on in horror, Dr. Prescott's entire body seemed to just dissolve away. Only her scorched and tattered clothing was left behind.

Later that day we told Elena's father everything that had happened. He reacted to our horrifying story with amazing calm. Apparently he, too, had suspected that a vampire had been responsible for the series of unexplained deaths but, as Elena had said, he could not voice such a theory for fear of losing his professional reputation. When we were done, he told us not to discuss the case with anyone and officially labeled Dr. Prescott's death as "accidental."

Life on Colony Four appeared to return to normal. There were no more mysterious deaths and no more rumors of supernatural forces roaming among us.

That is, until Elena told me some chilling news. The body of Dr. Kessler, Prescott's first victim and the only corpse not yet sent back to Earth, had disappeared from the morgue. A colony-wide search had revealed no trace of it.

Sitting in the food court, staring out at the holographic mountains, a horrible thought ran through my mind. If my memory was correct, vampires reproduced by biting humans and infecting them with their cursed blood. If so, there was a chance that Kessler had returned from the dead. Like our endless days and equally endless nights, our nightmare would not be over for a long, long time.

Blood Sisters

———

Leslie Gordon and Marcia Sackett had been best friends for as long as either of them could remember. They were born just two days apart, and their families had moved to Eden Lane within a week of one another. The girls had gone to the same preschool and shared the same doctor. They went to the same dentist, and had been lucky enough to have been in the same classes from kindergarten all the way through eighth grade.

Whatever one girl did, the other did, too. When Leslie decided to join the Campfire Girls, Marcia immediately signed up as well. When Marcia got her ears pierced on her twelfth birthday, so did Leslie. They even got the chicken pox at exactly the same time.

Leslie and Marcia shared clothes, homework, and secrets. When they were eleven years old, during a sleepover at Marcia's house, they vowed to be best friends for life—and for whatever life might await them in the hereafter. The girls wrote down a solemn oath, recited it, and sealed the vow with double scoops of mint-chip ice cream.

It was a promise that Leslie would live to regret.

* * *

The trouble began during their first week of eighth grade when the girls decided to try out for their junior high school's cheerleading squad. They agreed it would be a great way to make new friends . . . *and* meet boys.

For an entire week before the tryouts, Leslie and Marcia practiced a series of original cheers, steps, and acrobatic routines. When the day of the auditions came, they wore identical outfits and performed their routines as a team.

Crystal Ballantine, captain of the cheerleading squad and, without a doubt, the most popular girl at Garfield Junior High, was quite impressed. However, no girl was *ever* allowed to join the squad without first passing one of Crystal's famous initiations.

"Initiation?" Leslie asked when she heard the news. "What's that?"

"It's like a test," Crystal explained. "We give you a challenge to prove you're worthy of being a cheerleader."

"We can do that," Marcia said immediately. "What would you like us to do?"

"Let me think," Crystal said, looking to Shannon McHugh, her second-in-command, for ideas. Crystal's recent initiations had included doing a week's worth of homework for the current squad members, polishing their bicycles, and taking them all out for pizza. Once, when she was feeling particularly nasty, she made a would-be cheerleader shave her head before making the squad. (This did not go over well with the girl's parents, nor with the school administration.)

"Make them clean our bedrooms," Shannon suggested.

Crystal shook her head. "Too easy."

"How about we make them double-date my twin brothers?" Shannon then said with a nasty giggle. Shannon's brothers, Ned and Fred, were two of the most disgusting boys in school. Just thinking about sitting next to them made Marcia feel like throwing up.

"No. I just got a C-minus on a science test, and I'm feeling *particularly* mean," Crystal said with a sneer, making sure that Leslie and Marcia knew she meant every word. "Hey, I know! How about they have to spend the night in Dracula's Castle?"

Dracula's Castle was the name the kids had given to an old abandoned mansion at the end of Cedar Street on the far edge of town. Empty for as long as any of them could remember, the house—built sometime in the early 1900s—not only looked as dark and creepy as a house could, but was rumored to be inhabited by an actual vampire. The story got started several years back when a number of dogs, cats, squirrels, and raccoons were discovered around the property, completely drained of blood.

"Perfect," said Shannon. She turned and smiled at Leslie and Marcia, whose faces had suddenly gone white. "A night in Dracula's Castle it is."

Pom-poms in hand, Leslie and Marcia walked home in silence. It wasn't until they reached the front door of Leslie's house that Marcia finally found the courage to speak.

"Maybe this isn't such a good idea after all," Marcia said. "I mean, who cares if we're cheerleaders, anyway?"

"*You* care, and so do I," Leslie insisted. "Crystal and Shannon are just trying to bully us, just like they try to bully every other girl at school. Well, they can't scare us. We'll take their stupid old initiation, and we'll pass it. Nothing can hurt us as long as we stick together. Right?"

Marcia was uncomfortably silent.

"*Right*?" Leslie repeated.

"Right," Marcia finally replied, obviously lying.

"All right, then," Leslie said. "You tell your folks that you're staying over at my place tonight, and I'll tell my folks that I'm staying at yours. We'll meet Crystal and Shannon at Dracula's Castle at nine o'clock, just like we promised. Deal?"

Marcia hesitated for a second, then smiled. "Deal," she said. "But if we get caught, killed, or bitten by anything, I want you to remember that I was totally against this!"

* * *

As arranged, all four girls met in front of the abandoned house at exactly nine o'clock that night. The sky was overcast, which made the dark old mansion with its gray stone walls, vine-covered turrets, and decaying roof look even spookier than usual. Leslie and Marcia had each brought a sleeping bag and flashlight. Shannon smiled evilly as Crystal gave them their instructions.

"You both have to stay in the house until seven

o'clock tomorrow morning," the squad captain explained. "If either one of you leaves before that, you're both disqualified. You're in this together. Got it?"

"All for one and one for all," Leslie declared.

"Exactly," Crystal said.

"How will you know we really stayed the entire time?" Marcia asked.

Crystal pointed to a house in the middle of the next block. "That's Shannon's house," she said. "Every hour on the hour you have to blink your flashlights three times from inside the house. If Shannon doesn't see your signal, you're out."

"You mean, you're going to stay up *all night*?" Marcia asked Shannon.

"No. My alarm is set to wake me up once during the night. But you don't know when, and you can't afford to take any chances," Shannon explained with a dark laugh.

"But that means *we* have to stay up all night!" Leslie protested.

"Trade off. Sleep in shifts. You'll work it out," Crystal said with a shrug. "That is, if you really want to be cheerleaders."

"We do," Leslie stated. She turned to Marcia. "Let's go."

Picking up her sleeping bag and taking her best friend by the arm, Leslie started up the cracked, weed-covered walk to Dracula's Castle. Giggling, Crystal and Shannon headed back down the street.

"Are you really going to get up in the middle of the night to watch for their signal?" Crystal asked her friend.

25

"No way," Shannon scoffed. "But *they* don't know that!"

Leslie and Marcia found the front door locked. However, since the neighborhood kids regularly used the house's windows for target practice, there were several broken ones to climb through.

Once inside, they gripped each other tightly as they moved fearfully through the dark, musty old mansion and looked for a place to sleep.

Finally Marcia shined her flashlight into the foyer. "Let's sleep next to the door," she said. "There's no rule that says we can't sleep near an easy way out."

"Good idea," Leslie agreed. "But we'd better unlock the door. I'm more afraid of what's inside this place than anything outside."

They quickly spread their sleeping bags out on the dusty hardwood floor and climbed inside them. Leslie looked at her watch. "It's nine-thirty. I'll take the first shift," she said. "You get some sleep, and I'll wake you at midnight. Then you let me sleep for a couple of hours, okay?"

"Okay," said Marcia. She settled into her sleeping bag, wondering if she actually *could* sleep in this creepy old place. But despite her fears, fifteen minutes later she was fast asleep.

While her friend rested peacefully, Leslie sat upright, her eyes and ears attuned to every creak, groan, and rustle coming from within the musty old mansion. Once, she was certain she heard something moving in the far corner of the room. When she shined her flashlight in the direction of the sound, she saw two beady red eyes staring back at her. Gasping and clutching her throat, Leslie almost screamed . . . until she saw that it was just a field mouse. More scared of her than she was of it, the mouse turned and scampered back into the darkness. Leslie let out a huge sigh of relief, then looked at her watch to see how much more time she had till midnight. She saw that it was only ten o'clock.

"Great," she said, groaning. "Two more hours!" And then she remembered that she had to signal Shannon every hour on the hour.

Walking over to a large, grime-covered window, she pointed her flashlight directly at Shannon's distant house and blinked the light three times. There was no return signal. Leslie wondered if Shannon was even bothering to look. Either way it made no difference. She had to follow instructions or risk having both Marcia and herself kicked off the cheerleading squad.

The next two hours passed with only the usual moans and pops of a creaky old house to keep Leslie company. At midnight, barely able to keep her eyes open, she flashed her signal, then gently shook her friend awake.

"Hey, Marcia, wake up," Leslie said softly.

Marcia's eyes instantly snapped open.

"Huh? What's wrong?" Marcia asked, confused.

"Nothing. It's midnight. Time for you to keep watch."

Marcia sat up painfully and tried to adjust her eyes to the darkness.

"All right," she said, still groggy. "Give me my flashlight. Try to get some sleep."

"Remember, you have to signal Shannon at one

27

o'clock and two o'clock. Then you can wake me up," said Leslie, sliding into her sleeping bag.

"No problem," Marcia said with a yawn. "Sweet dreams."

Leslie turned over on her side, shut her eyes, and took a long, deep breath. *This isn't going to be so hard after all,* she thought.

She was just beginning to drift off when she heard Marcia whisper, "Leslie. Leslie, wake up!"

Alarmed, Leslie sat up and turned to her friend.

"What is it?" she asked.

"I have to go to the bathroom," Marcia said.

"What?" asked Leslie in disbelief.

"*I have to go to the bathroom,*" Marcia insisted. "What do I do?"

"I don't know," Leslie said. "There must be a bathroom around here somewhere."

"Come with me," Marcia pleaded.

"All right," Leslie agreed, reluctantly climbing out of her sleeping bag into the cold, damp air of the dark house.

Arm in arm, Leslie and Marcia nervously wandered into the heart of Dracula's Castle. Their flashlight beams punched through the inky darkness, revealing room after room empty of anything but the dust and debris left from decades of neglect. There was no bathroom in sight.

They had made it all the way back to the house's enormous kitchen when a loud creaking sound—like the opening of an ancient coffin—caused them both to freeze in their tracks.

"What was that?" Marcia asked, squeezing Leslie's

arm so hard that her nails nearly cut into her friend's skin.

"My m-mother would say it was pr-probably just the house settling," Leslie stammered.

Thomp-thomp-thomp. The house was now filled with the unmistakable sound of heavy footsteps.

"I'm not sure what a house does when it's settling," Marcia moaned, "but I don't think that's it."

"Crystal? Shannon?" Leslie barely managed to squeak out. "If you're trying to scare us, it's not going to work."

The sound of footfalls ceased. Breathing in short, shallow gasps, the girls strained to hear more but the house remained eerily silent.

"Probably just a tree hitting the side of the house," Leslie said softly.

"Right," Marcia agreed. "Probably just a tree."

They turned to continue their search—only to find a man standing directly in front of them. Over six feet tall, he was completely bald and had gray, bloodless skin. His red, ratlike eyes glistened in the darkness, and when he smiled, he revealed two long snakelike fangs.

"You have trespassed on cursed ground," the creature growled. "And now you are *mine!*"

The vampire's breath was strong and foul, like the smell of a rotting corpse. His entire body carried the stench of death.

Locking eyes with the vampire, Leslie and Marcia screamed with all the power in their lungs. Then they turned and bolted, racing headlong for the front door.

Leslie was the first to get there. Not even bothering

to grab her sleeping bag, she threw open the door, leaped off the porch, and stumbled down the broken walkway to the edge of Cedar Street. Only then did she pause to look back for her friend.

"Marcia!" she called, turning back toward the evil old house. "Marcia! Where are you?" But there was no reply. Marcia was nowhere to be seen.

For a brief moment Leslie considered returning to the mansion. But she knew that would be suicide. If the vampire had captured Marcia—or worse—he'd have no trouble getting Leslie, too. No, she couldn't do this alone. She needed help. She needed to call the police.

Shannon's house was the closest, so Leslie raced for it and banged furiously on the front door. Shannon's father answered. He was naturally surprised to find his daughter's classmate standing on his porch in the middle of the night babbling tearfully about vampires and missing girls.

At Leslie's insistence the police were called, but a nightlong search failed to turn up any trace of either Marcia or the vampire Leslie insisted had abducted her. Leslie was taken home, given a sleeping pill to help her rest, and she remained asleep until the middle of the following afternoon.

Days passed without any news about Marcia or her fate. An investigation into Crystal and Shannon's initiations was launched. Both girls were forced to quit the cheerleading squad and were suspended from school. Leslie herself refused to go back to school. She barely managed to leave her bedroom, constantly reliving in her mind her experience in Dracula's Castle.

Then, five days after Marcia's disappearance, Leslie

was lying in her bed trying to fall asleep when she heard a familiar voice call to her.

"Leslie? Leslie?"

A chill ran down Leslie's spine. The voice seemed faint and far away. Could she be dreaming?

"Leslie, over here! It's me! Marcia!"

Leslie bolted up in bed and looked around her room. No one was there.

"Over here!" the voice called. "At the window!"

Leslie slowly climbed out of bed, carefully walked to her bedroom window, and pulled back the curtain.

And then she screamed like she'd never screamed before. Framed in the window, not two feet away from her, was the face of her dearest friend in the world, Marcia Sackett! She looked gray and bloodless, like the face of the vampire that had ambushed them in the old mansion. And like the vampire, Marcia's eyes glowed with an eerie red light.

For a moment Leslie wondered how Marcia—or what had once *been* Marcia—had managed to climb up the side of her house to the second floor. And then she realized that Marcia was actually *floating* in the air outside her window, her body suspended fifteen feet above the grass-covered lawn below by some kind of supernatural forces.

"Marcia?" Leslie gasped in disbelief.

"Yes, it's me, Leslie. Don't you recognize your best friend?" the Marcia/vampire said in a strange singsong voice. "Aren't you going to let me in? We have so much to talk about."

"No," Leslie said with a shudder. "Go away! You're not Marcia. You *can't* be."

"But I *am* Marcia," the young vampire insisted. "And I miss you. Why did you run away and leave me behind? You promised we'd be together for ever and ever."

"But . . . but I didn't leave you!" Leslie wailed. "We were running together. I thought you were right behind me."

"It's so hard to talk this way," Marcia said, running her pale, gray hand over the glass. "Open the window and let me in."

Leslie almost did exactly that, but then she remembered something she'd seen in an old horror movie—vampires can't enter a home unless they're invited in.

"No," she said firmly, pulling her hand away from the lock. "I—I can't. You're . . . *different* now, Marcia. Don't you see that?"

"All right, Leslie," Marcia said sadly. "I'll go away . . . for now." And then she smiled, revealing a set of razor-sharp fangs. "But I'll be back. We're still best friends, you know. We took an oath to be best friends for ever and ever."

With a chilling laugh, Marcia turned away and vanished in a cloud of mist. For a long time Leslie just stood there at the window, terrified that Marcia—or, more accurately, the thing that Marcia had become—would return. It was another hour before she found the courage to turn away from the window and climb back into her bed. And it was another hour after that before she finally slipped into a shallow, fitful sleep.

As she promised, Marcia did return to Leslie's window the next night, and the night after that, too.

Throughout high school and college, Leslie's nights were plagued by the ghostly appearances of her undead friend who herself never aged. Even after Leslie graduated from college and traveled all the way to Australia to make her new home, Marcia followed, always appearing exactly at midnight and always asking to be invited in.

After all, Leslie and Marcia had promised to be best friends in life, and in whatever life awaited them in the hereafter. And Marcia would never let Leslie forget her promise.

A Campfire Story

silvery half-moon slid out from behind a patch of thin, gray clouds, and somewhere off in the distant woods a lone wolf bayed woefully. The night was alive with sounds—the rhythmic chirping of crickets, the throaty croaking of frogs, the steady drone of insects, and the occasional flutter of bat wings.

In a small clearing four figures gathered around a blazing campfire. One was a man, about thirty-five to forty years old with a handsome, rugged face topped by a thick mane of wavy black hair. Another was a woman, also in her mid-thirties, with fine, delicate features and long, straight hair the color of midnight. The remaining two were their children, a boy of perhaps thirteen and a girl a few years younger. Both had their mother's delicate skin and their father's proud, regal bearing.

Dressed in lightweight jackets, the family sat around the fire, warming their hands. They looked quite content, having just eaten a hearty meal in the great outdoors.

"It's getting late," the father said. "Almost time to get ready for bed."

"Do we have to?" the son whined. "We're having so much fun."

"You know how important it is for young people to get their rest," his mother reminded him. "We've got a big hike planned for tomorrow, and you need your sleep."

"Can we have a story first, Father?" the daughter asked.

"Yes! A story!" her brother chimed in. "And make it a scary one!"

"We love scary stories!" the girl agreed.

The father looked at his beautiful wife and smiled. Their children were so excited about hearing one of their dad's famous horror stories that it was almost impossible to say no.

"All right, children," the father said, turning up the collar of his jacket. "But just one story. Then you have to promise to go right to sleep."

"We promise," the children said in unison.

"All right, now let me think," the father said. He crept a few inches closer to the fire and looked into the wild, dancing flames. The children watched him closely, eager with anticipation.

"Once upon a time," their father began slowly, "great monsters roamed the earth."

"Monsters?" the son gasped. "What kind of monsters?"

"Were they big and hairy?" the daughter asked nervously. "And did they have six arms and big bug eyes?"

"No, darling. Those were the monsters in my last story," her father explained, his voice low and calm. "For the most part, these monsters looked just like us. But if you looked closer, you could see that their faces were dark and hard, and the cores of their eyes were as black as midnight."

The man paused a moment to allow his children to fix this frightening image in their minds.

"These monsters hated normal people and wanted to kill us all and claim this world for their own," he continued. "Over the centuries these cowardly creatures hunted us down and murdered us mercilessly in our sleep."

The boy and girl gasped at the thought of such vicious killings and huddled closer together for protection.

"These monsters were not as strong as us, but they had many special powers," the father said. "They could go for days without sleep. They could eat virtually anything. And there were so many of them that they soon spread throughout the planet like a great plague. All of us were in great danger."

"What happened to these monsters, Father?" the boy asked, his eyes wide.

"Well, over many, many years our population grew, and soon we were able to fight back," the father said. "From street to street, from town to town, and from country to country, we moved like an army, vanquishing this vile scourge from the earth. Finally, after decades of battle, only a handful of the monsters remained. But these survivors proved to be the most dangerous of all. In fact, one almost killed *me*."

"No!" the girl gasped. "You were almost killed by a monster?"

Her father nodded gravely. "It was a night I will never forget."

"Tell us how it happened," the boy said, inching his way closer to the fire.

"It was a year or so before I met your mother," the father said in the same even, spooky tone. "I was still a student at the university and was living in an old apartment building. There had been a number of mysterious deaths in the area, and I began to hear rumors of a deadly monster who killed people in their sleep."

"What did you do?" the boy inquired.

"Well, at first I dismissed these rumors as fairy tales," his father said. "After all, I believed the monsters had died off years ago."

He paused to throw some fresh wood on the dying fire. The branches crackled and sparked as they burst into flame, then settled down to emit a warm, steady light.

The man continued with his story. "However, one evening I was awakened from my sleep by a horrific scream from somewhere in the building. I immediately leaped to my feet and ran to the front door, listening for any further cries. I heard the scream again . . . closer this time. In fact, it seemed to be coming from the apartment directly across the hall. So I reached for the knob, opened my door—"

"No!" the boy shouted. "What if the monster had been there? You could have been killed!"

"I know," the father said. "But I still didn't believe

there was a monster in the building. All I knew was that my neighbor was in trouble, and I had to help. Anyway, I opened the door and ran to the apartment across the hall. I could hear struggling inside. Summoning all my strength, I slammed my shoulder against the door and knocked it down."

Again the man paused, studying the tense faces of his two children.

"Well, don't leave us hanging," his wife said. "Tell us what you saw."

"My neighbor, a young man named Anton, lay dead on the floor," the man said slowly. "A wooden stake was sticking out of his chest."

"No!" the boy gasped in horror.

"There was a monster standing over him," the father went on. "In its hand was a large wooden mallet. The monster had crept into Anton's bedroom and slaughtered him according to the ancient rituals. This thing then turned and looked at me, and I will never forget the look of pure hatred in its eyes."

"What did you do, Father?" the little girl asked nervously. "Did you run?"

"No, I didn't run. The thought didn't even occur to me," her father responded. "All I knew was that, standing there facing this ancient evil, I had to act. I had to kill this beast where it stood or more of my brothers would be killed. And their deaths would be my fault."

The father paused for a moment to collect his thoughts, then continued speaking in slow, measured tones.

"I launched myself at the monster, my fangs aimed

straight at its throat," said the father dramatically. "But it swung its mallet, catching me across the side of my face and knocking me to the ground. By the time I recovered from the blow, it had scurried from the room and disappeared down the stairs."

The two children gazed at their father in silent wonder. Finally the boy spoke.

"Is that it?" he asked, his voice clearly conveying disappointment. "That's the whole story about you and the monster?"

"Oh, no, my son," the father said with a knowing laugh. "That was just the beginning. Since I had seen the monster and lived, I was now a danger to it. And since it knew where I lived, it could come for me whenever it wanted. Obviously I could not avoid sleep forever. So I had to track this murderous creature down and kill it before it killed me."

The father's face turned grim, and his gaze became distant as a flood of unpleasant memories washed over him.

"With only three hours left until sunrise, I quickly tried to figure out where the monster might be hiding," he explained. "I ruled out my own apartment building, since there was no way his kind could live there undetected. Going outside, I sniffed the air and soon found his vile scent. I followed it for three blocks until I came to an abandoned twelve-story office tower."

As his children listened with rapt attention, the father explained how he transformed himself into a bat and flew to the top of the office building where he believed the monster was hiding.

"I found footing on a metal ledge no more than four

inches wide," he said, measuring the short distance with his hands. "Then, with my body pressed against the grime-covered glass, I peered into the dark offices inside. Supposedly this building had been empty for years, but I could make out clear signs that someone had recently been living there. Aluminum cans were strewn about, as were the rotting remains of fruits and vegetables."

"I *hate* vegetables!" the boy exclaimed, scrunching up his face.

"What happened next?" the girl pleaded. "Did the monster appear?"

"It certainly did," her father replied. "At first I saw only a shadow along the far wall. Then a blinding flashlight beam cut through the darkness, and behind it appeared the monster that had murdered Anton. It immediately saw me and shined the flashlight beam directly into my eyes, momentarily blinding me. It then grabbed a handgun from a desk and fired the weapon directly at me, which, of course, caused me no harm whatsoever. However, the impact of the bullets on the glass caused the window to shatter into a million jagged pieces. With the glass gone, I could now enter the monster's lair."

The father's voice grew louder and more intense as he described his terrifying confrontation with evil.

"I leaped into the room and bared my fangs, ready to attack," he said, jumping to his feet as he spoke. "The air was filled with the scent of the monster's hot blood as it pumped rapidly through its corrupted heart. And there was the wretched smell of something else, too. But before I realized what it was, I felt a ring of fire burning into my neck."

"No, Father, not garlic!" the little girl howled, burying her face in her hands.

"Yes, a whole rope of the awful cloves—and the monster had tightened them around my throat."

"How did you escape?" the boy asked nervously.

"Well, at first I merely thrashed about, trying to free the garlic rope from my neck. But the monster had jumped onto my back and there seemed no way to shake it off," the father said. "And all this time it kept shouting, 'Die, you devil, die!'"

"How rude," the mother scoffed.

"Finally, with my energy rapidly draining, I did the only thing I could do," the father said, his voice filled with emotion. "I summoned all my remaining strength and pitched myself *backward* through the shattered window."

"How brave you were, my darling!" the mother exclaimed.

Looking a bit bashful, the father went on to tell the thrilling conclusion of his story.

"We fell together, the monster and I, the wind howling in my ears as the ground rocketed toward us. And then, just before we were both smashed like insects, the monster released me. At the same time, the garlic rope slipped off from around my throat and, thankfully, my strength returned. With only seconds left before I would have slammed into the pavement, I managed to once again transform myself into a bat and fly to safety."

"And the monster?" the boy asked eagerly. "What happened to it?"

"Monsters never learned to fly," his father said with a smile. "There wasn't much left of it after it hit the sidewalk."

"Hooray!" the children cheered.

"After that, the killings in our neighborhood stopped. And all the vampires were able to live happily ever after," the man concluded. "Of course, some say that a few monsters still roam the earth. They hunt by day, determined to hammer a stake through the heart of every sleeping vampire in the land. In fact, I've heard stories of monsters living in these very woods. Monsters with warm skin and cold eyes. Monsters who look just like . . . *that!*"

He pointed directly over the children's shoulders. The boy and girl turned and screamed . . . only to see the golden eyes of a barn owl blinking at them from a nearby tree branch.

"Ooops. Sorry," the father said with an impish laugh. "I couldn't resist."

"That's quite enough, dear," his wife said. "All right now, kids. You've had your spooky story. It's almost sunrise. It's time to go to sleep."

"Good day, Mother," the boy said. "Good day, Father."

"Good day, Father, Mother," the girl repeated, giving each of her parents a kiss on the cheek.

And with that, as the first rays of dawn poked above the eastern horizon, the family members climbed into their cozy camping coffins.

Just before drifting off, the sister reached over and knocked on her big brother's coffin. He lifted the lid and poked his head out.

"What?" he asked.

"Do you think Father's story is true? Do you think he really killed a monster?" she whispered.

"No way," the boy replied. "Everyone knows there's no such thing as monsters."

Then they both lay in their coffins, closed their eyes, and drifted off to enjoy a good day's sleep.

A Fate Worse Than Death

———

I still remember the flash. It was ten-thirty on Wednesday morning, and I was in Mr. Weston's third period science class. We were studying basic chemistry. He was having us perform a series of experiments designed to show how, when heated together, certain chemicals can combine to form different, often unusual compounds.

I was boiling a greenish liquid over a Bunsen burner. My lab partner, a geek named Lester McGraw, strolled over to me and pulled a small packet of gray powder out of his shirt pocket.

"Hey, Jenny, want to see some real fireworks?" he asked with his usual goofball laugh. Lester was always trying to impress me with one stunt or another. I think he liked me. I didn't want to hurt the poor nerd's feelings, but sometimes it took a real effort just to be pleasant to the irritating little dweeb.

"No, thanks. Lester. Let's just concentrate on doing

the experiment, okay?" I said, sighing, my patience already running short.

"No, really, you're going to love this," Lester insisted, pushing me aside. Then, before I could stop him, he poured the gray powder into our beaker. Immediately the boiling green liquid turned a deep blood red. Tiny little sparks, like miniature fireflies, flashed for a moment, then disappeared.

"Pretty cool, huh?" Lester said with glee, his laugh a mulish bray. "That's called *thermophosphorescence*."

"That's very nice, Lester," I said coolly. "But now you've ruined our experiment. We have to start all over again."

"That's okay, Jen. I'll do it," Lester offered, reaching for the Bunsen burner controls. But at that moment Mr. Weston walked by and noticed the odd-colored liquid in our beaker.

"What is *that*?" he asked with curiosity. "The compound is supposed to be green."

I shot Lester a look that could kill an entire busload of geeks.

"Well?" Mr. Weston demanded sternly, his arms folded across his chest. "Would either of you care to explain this to me?"

Before I could respond, Lester stepped forward. "Sir, I cannot tell a lie," he declared as if he was trying out for the school's Presidents' Day pageant. "It was I who altered our experiment. You see, I just got this sample of powdered magnesium tri-benzoate and—"

"My goodness! What's happening?" Mr. Weston cried, pointing at the beaker.

I turned and saw that the once-reddish liquid was

now a swirling mass of colors ranging from pumpkin orange to indigo blue. Within this abstract nightmare of colors, thousands of twinkling lights were exploding like tiny flashbulbs.

"Look!" I shouted, pointing not at the beaker but at the Bunsen burner flame burning brightly beneath it. Apparently this increase in chemical activity was occurring because Lester had accidentally turned the flame *higher* instead of turning it off. Now, instead of causing a simple chemical reaction, he'd set off an uncontrolled chain reaction!

"Whoa!" Lester yelped, beaming. "Those colors are way cool!"

"Stand back, you idiot!" I yelled, reaching past Lester to shut off the flame myself. But I was too late. The beaker vibrated violently, then exploded, sending a brilliant flash—as bright as the noonday sun—right into my eyes.

The next thing I knew I was staring up into the blue autumn sky.

"It's all right, Jenny," said a man I'd never seen before as he looked down at me from what seemed to be a million miles away. "Just close your eyes and rest. You're going to be okay."

I tried to move but found that I was strapped firmly into place . . . and rising into the air!

"Hey, what's going on?" I whispered weakly as I was loaded into the back of an ambulance. Then the heavy metal doors slammed shut at my feet and a siren wailed as I fell into what felt like a black hole.

Time became impossible to track as I drifted in and out of consciousness. I remember arriving at a hospital emergency room, where there was chaotic activity with a lot of running and shouting, and I remember somebody putting a heavy rubber mask over my face. I smelled a foul, stale odor, and the next thing I knew it was nighttime and I was lying in a dimly lit recovery room. I tried to sit up but found I was too weak to move. So I just lay there, trying to make sense of it all until a middle-aged nurse happened to peer into my room and noticed that I was staring at her.

"She's awake, Dr. Cannon," I heard her whisper excitedly. A few minutes later a handsome young doctor arrived and sat by my side.

"Hi, Jenny. My name is Dr. Cannon," he said with a smile. "How are you feeling?"

"Awful," I moaned. "Where am I?"

"At Mercy General Hospital. You were brought in here six days ago following an accident in your school chemistry lab. Do you remember that?" he asked, gently pulling my eyelids back.

"Yeah, I remember," I groaned. "Tell Lester McGraw I'm going to kill him."

Dr. Cannon pulled out a small penlight and shined it into my right eye. "Ouch!" I screamed as I jerked my head away. It felt like someone had just jabbed a pin into my eyeball.

"I'm sorry but you're going to have to hold still," Dr. Cannon said as he shined the beam at my eye a second time.

"But that light *hurts*!" I yelled. "Keep it away from me!"

Dr. Cannon gave a frustrated grunt and pocketed the penlight. His worried expression told me that something was seriously amiss.

"So what's wrong with me?" I asked pointedly. Then I looked around the otherwise empty room. "Where are my parents? Why aren't they here?"

"We sent your parents home so they could get some rest. We had no idea how long it would take for you to regain consciousness, and they had been here for days," Dr. Cannon said. "As for your condition, that's a bit more difficult to explain."

"Do I look like a freak?" I asked in horror, thinking that would truly be a fate worse than death.

"No, Jenny, you look fine," Dr. Cannon replied. "Unfortunately, when the explosion occurred, some flying glass cut your arm, exposing your blood to the chemical vapors."

"Yeah? So?" I asked, still not liking where this conversation was going.

"We haven't fully analyzed the chemicals involved, but they appear to have reacted with your DNA to cause a rare form of anemia," Dr. Cannon explained. "It's a condition that affects your blood's ability to get nourishment to your body. Until we can get this condition under control, you're going to need regular blood supplements, and you'll probably be hypersensitive to bright lights."

"How long will it take to get this condition under control?" I asked, feeling a cold chill growing in the pit of my stomach.

"That's difficult to say," Dr. Cannon replied, scratching his chin in deep thought. "As I said before, this type of condition is extremely rare, and the literature on it is pretty thin."

For a brief moment my mind was filled with

cascading images of doctors, nurses, needles, tubes, and endless hours of painful poking, prodding, and blood tests. Then, as I turned to look up at the strong, warm face of Dr. Cannon, another thought occurred to me: *I really don't need all those needles and tests. All I need is your blood!*

Don't ask me why, but I suddenly had this crazy impulse to bite Dr. Cannon's neck and drain him of every drop of blood in his body. It was as if I was responding to some deep, ancient instinct that was only now beginning to awaken within me. And oddly enough it felt as natural as a hungry kid craving a chocolate bar, or a shipwrecked person dying for a drink of lifesaving water.

"Dr. Cannon," I said, my voice a soft whisper. "Come closer. I need to tell you something."

Dr. Cannon bent down.

"Closer," I said as if I could barely summon the strength to speak.

He leaned closer still. Suddenly I could actually smell the rich, warm blood coursing through the man's jugular vein not two inches from my lips. The delicious aroma caused my heart to thunder in my chest and my stomach to literally ache with hunger. I ran my tongue across my upper teeth and felt a sharp sting as it passed over my canine teeth. Instantly I knew why . . . they had grown into two-inch-long fangs.

Moving in a sudden, unexpected burst of speed, I reached up and grabbed Dr. Cannon's head, pulling him toward me. I opened my mouth, sighed with anticipation, and plunged my newly formed fangs deep into the side of his neck.

The doctor screamed and struggled to break free, but some previously untapped source of strength suddenly exploded inside me. I, a thirteen-year-old former weakling, held Dr. Cannon in place as if he were as weak and powerless as a puppy. There was no way he could escape.

And then I drank. And it tasted good. It was like a chocolate shake, a sweet fruit punch, and a refreshing glass of mountain spring water all rolled into one. Each mouthful filled my body with feelings of enormous warmth, strength, and well-being. And suddenly I felt like I could do *anything*!

The nurse, who had been standing watching this scene in utter horror, suddenly found her legs and turned to run. I released Dr. Cannon's lifeless body and threw myself at her. Well, I didn't actually throw myself at her . . . I *flew* at her. I mean, I literally jumped right out of bed and sailed at least fifteen feet across the room and landed directly on the nurse's back. Then, as if they had a mind of their own, my fangs sank hungrily into the woman's neck. Screaming, she fell to the floor, and once again I drank from the wellspring of life until I could drink no more.

Finished, I stepped over the nurse's lifeless body and cautiously looked out into the dimly lit hospital corridor. My newfound instincts told me that I had to run, that I had to hide, that humanity and I were now at war.

Throwing on Dr. Cannon's blood-splattered lab coat and slipping on the nurse's white sneakers, I moved out into the hall and headed for the distant elevators. Along the way I passed two nurses who threw me only a passing glance before continuing on their way. Apparently the sight of someone covered with blood hurrying through the hospital hallways was not particularly unusual.

I soon reached the elevators and hit the "down" button. As I waited impatiently for the elevator to arrive, I happened to glance at a mirror on the nearby wall. What I saw shocked me. Or, more accurately, what I *didn't* see. Although the bloodstained doctor's coat was clearly visible, I wasn't. In the mirror's reflection it looked as if the coat was suspended in midair. I immediately looked at my hands. They were still there. I was visible to myself and everyone else, but I didn't have a reflection!

I was still staring at the mirror in silent awe when the elevator arrived. Luckily it was empty. I quickly jumped inside, pushed the button for the lobby, and immediately began my descent, giggling with glee all the way down. Clearly this change in my DNA had affected me both physically and mentally. I was no longer just cute little Jennifer Samuels. No, now I was someone *better.* I was someone *dangerous.* I was someone to be *respected.*

Leaving the hospital, I considered going home, then immediately dismissed that idea. My parents were always complaining that they didn't know how to handle a growing thirteen-year-old girl. If they couldn't cope with me before, they'd have absolutely *no* chance with me now. Instead I decided to pay a visit to the one person who most deserved to get a taste of the powers I now enjoyed—Lester McGraw.

Moving swiftly through the night with the strength

and grace of a jungle cat, I considered the delicious irony of my plan. Lester had made me the person I now was, so it was only fitting that he see firsthand what he had created. After tonight, Lester would never pester me again.

I arrived at Lester's house in seconds, even though he lived at least seven blocks from the hospital. It was so cool. I didn't actually run—I sort of glided, and I wasn't even breathing hard! Whatever this "condition" was, it certainly had its benefits.

Sniffing the air, I could sense Lester lying in the bedroom just beyond the third set of windows on the house's second floor. Bending low, I gathered my newfound strength, leaped into the air, and instantly found myself perched on the narrow windowsill outside his room. It was as easy as hopping up onto someone's front porch.

Unfortunately, getting inside his room didn't look like it was going to be quite so easy. Lester's window was closed. Despite the dim light, I could see Lester sleeping in his bed as clearly as if it was daytime, since my sight, like the rest of my senses, had grown as sharp as my new fangs. Standing there, I wanted to wrench the window open and climb inside, but I felt something preventing me from doing so. I instinctively knew that I would not be able to enter Lester's house until someone let me in.

"Lester! Hey, Lester!" I whispered at the sleeping figure on the other side of the windowpane. "Lester, wake up!"

Not five feet away, Lester stirred, rolled over, and looked sleepily in my direction. He tried to focus his nearsighted eyes on the window.

"Hi, Lester," I cooed softly. "You wanna come out and play?"

"Jenny?" Lester looked confused. He reached over to his nightstand and fumbled for his glasses, knocking over a glass of water in the process. Sliding them onto his beaky nose, he whispered, "Jenny? What are you doing out *there*?"

"I came to see you, Lester," I said with a smile. "I wanted you to know I was all right. Can you let me in? It's kinda cold out here."

Lester threw back his covers—I could see they were printed with a geeky spaceship design—and rushed over to the window. He reached for the latch, prepared to open the window, then stopped.

"Are you sure you're okay?" he asked suspiciously. "Why is your jacket all covered with blood?"

"I had a nosebleed," I said with forced sincerity. "Now, come on, Lester. Open the window before I fall off the ledge."

"But how did you get up here in the first place?" Lester asked, looking past me toward the ground below.

"With a ladder," I replied, my voice on edge.

"I don't see any ladder," Lester remarked.

"Just open the stupid window!" I yelled, my patience at an end. Then I added with a smile, "Please?"

Lester looked me over and appeared satisfied. He carefully opened the window and stood back to let me in. I stepped inside and jumped to the ground, keeping my face turned away from his. His innocence was positively pathetic! Anyone this stupid *deserved* to die!

"Thank you, Lester," I said cheerfully. I ran my tongue over my top teeth. Already I could feel my fangs beginning to grow and sharpen in eager anticipation of the feast ahead. "You have no idea how much this means to me."

Eyes ablaze, I spun around toward Lester, ready to strike. But instead of seeing his face frozen in terror, I saw only my bloodied lab coat reflected in the hand mirror he now held before him. The image held me spellbound.

"Hold it right there!" Lester commanded. "Come no closer, Queen of the Undead!"

Now, for the first time, I was able to discern the other images being reflected toward me in the mirror. There were posters on the wall behind me—all of them from classic horror movies. In addition, Lester had mounted photos of the most famous actors ever to play Count Dracula. *Just my luck,* I thought. *Lester McGraw is an expert on vampires!*

"How did you know I was a vampire?" I gasped, unable to believe that he'd identified my new nature so quickly.

"Getting up to my window without a ladder made me kind of suspicious," Lester explained. "But that red glow in your eyes was a real giveaway. So how did it happen, Jen? What turned you into a junior bloodsucker?"

"*You* did this to me," I growled angrily. "You and your stupid science experiment!"

"Then I guess you owe me," Lester said, giving me one of his horsy laughs.

"*Owe* you?" I snorted. "I should kill you!" I bared my fangs, eager to see the terror in his eyes.

"No, no, this is great!" Lester babbled on. "You get to live forever, you'll never get old, and you can turn into a bat whenever you want. It's the greatest thing in the world. In fact, here's what I want you to do. Give me a little nip . . . right here." He pointed to the side of his neck. "Turn me into a vampire, too. Then we can travel through eternity together!"

It took me a minute to really understand what Lester was saying. When I finally realized he wanted to live forever with me, the thought of laying my lips on Lester McGraw's flesh turned my stomach. The image of him and me as co-vampires sucking blood through the centuries was enough to make me want to plunge a stake through my *own* heart.

Holding my left arm in front of my face to block my view of the mirror, I lowered my head and ran back to the open window.

"Sorry, Lester, but I'm outta here," I said, jumping up onto the sill.

"You can run, but you can't hide forever, Jennifer Samuels!" Lester declared. "No matter how long it takes, I'll hunt you down. And when I do, we'll be together through eternity!"

He laughed again, that same awful bray. It was enough to set my vampire fangs on edge.

"You—you monster!" I screamed and launched myself into the night.

"No! Jenny!" Lester cried, running to the window. "Come back!" But he was too late. My arms had become leathery wings, and I was now beating them as hard as I could to get away from him.

In a flash, one freak of science had changed my life forever. As bad as that was, I wasn't going to have *this* freak of science make it worse.

So off I flew toward the full moon. On past the clouds, past the stars, on and on into endless oblivion. But no matter how far I flew, no matter how many years passed, no matter how many miles I put behind me, I knew I would never be safe. For out there, somewhere, would lurk a fate worse than undeath.

And his name was Lester McGraw.

Heirloom

➤

adine Barlow had never even *heard* of Great Aunt Lucille until the day her mother took her aside and told her that the woman had passed on. She hadn't quite known how to react to the news. Now, standing at the gravesite under a slow, steady rain, she felt even more uncomfortable. Fourteen years old, Nadine had been lucky enough to have never lost anyone close to her. To her, death was something that happened only on TV, in the movies, or to people you didn't really know. Even now, as she watched the polished wooden coffin being lowered into the ground, she felt nothing special for the person inside it. Supposedly Lucille was her mother's aunt, but since there had never been any contact between their families, she might as well have been from Mars as far as Nadine was concerned.

As the minister stood over the grave and read several passages from the Bible, Nadine took the opportunity to scan the faces of the thirty or so other mourners at the gravesite. Most of the people appeared to be at least fifty years old. The only exceptions were her older sister, Diane, and two teenage boys who looked like they desperately wanted to be somewhere else. Nadine was definitely the youngest person there. She took pride in the fact that she was able to look just as sad and depressed as any of the adults, even if she was only putting on an act.

As her eyes roamed over the rows of faces—some familiar, most not—Nadine noticed a tall, stern-looking man in his late thirties or early forties. He wore a dark trench coat over an equally dark wool suit, the kind men in old movies wore. He didn't seem to be paying attention to the ceremony. In fact, he was staring directly at *her* . . . and it wasn't a friendly gaze.

Creepy, Nadine thought, turning her eyes away from him. But even though she was no longer looking at the man, she continued to feel his gaze on her throughout the burial ceremony.

After what seemed like an eternity, the service was finally over. Slowly the guests said their good-byes and headed back to their cars. Walking with her parents and older sister, Nadine glanced back several times to see what the mysterious stranger was up to. He was slowly walking toward the narrow road where all the mourners' cars were parked. He walked alone without a single person approaching him or even giving him a passing wave. And as he walked, his eyes remained fixed on Nadine.

"Mom, who's that man looking at us?" she finally asked her mother, pointing to the man in the trench coat. Immediately the stranger turned away, concealing his face.

"I don't know," her mother said, peering through the misty fog that blanketed the cemetery. "He's probably a relative from out of town."

Nadine piled into the car with the rest of her family, and as they pulled away, she turned and looked out the back window. The stranger was standing by the roadside, still staring at her with his odd fixed gaze. Somehow, Nadine knew, it would not be the last time she'd see him.

A reception was held at the house of Nadine's Aunt Carole, her mother's older sister. It was a sumptuous affair, and Nadine stood by the food-laden tables, deciding what to eat. Just about everyone who had attended the service was there—except, thankfully, the dark stranger.

"Nadine?" asked a heavyset man with a round, kind face as he approached her with a plate overflowing with food. "My name is Barry Wilder. I was your great aunt Lucille's attorney."

"Nice to meet you, Mr. Wilder," Nadine said politely, extending her hand. She wondered what a lawyer would want with *her.*

"Did you know you were mentioned in your great aunt's will?" he asked, taking a bite from an onion roll stuffed with roast beef, lettuce, and mustard. "She wanted you to have something to remember her by."

"She did?" Nadine asked with surprise. "I didn't even know her."

"Perhaps not, but she certainly knew *you,*" the portly attorney replied, reaching awkwardly into the pocket of his navy blue suit jacket. "Enough that she instructed me, upon her death, to give you this."

Mr. Wilder pulled out a delicate gold chain. Hanging from the chain was a heart-shaped gold locket.

"It's beautiful!" Nadine exclaimed.

"And now it's yours," Mr. Wilder said with a smile as he dropped the locket gently into Nadine's outstretched hand. "I suggest you be very careful with it. It's an heirloom."

"*Heirloom*?" Nadine repeated. "What's that?"

"A valuable object that's passed down in a family from generation to generation," Mr. Wilder explained. "From what your great aunt told me before her death, that locket has been in your family for almost three hundred years."

Nadine carefully turned the locket in her hands as she examined it. It was heart-shaped and trimmed with fine, delicate engraving. There was a small clasp on the side of the heart, and when she pressed it, the locket popped open to reveal two tiny painted portraits inside. One picture was of a handsome young man dressed in the elegant style of the early eighteenth century. The other was of a pretty young woman who looked very much like . . . Nadine!

"Who's this girl?" Nadine asked with surprise. "She looks like me!"

"I know," Mr. Wilder said with a slightly uncomfortable laugh. "That's how I managed to recognize you so quickly. There is quite a strong family resemblance."

"But who is she?" Nadine repeated insistently. "We could almost be twins!"

"Your great-great-great-great something or other,"

Mr. Wilder said with a dismissive wave of his hand. "The young man on the other side is something of a mystery. Lucille never told me about him. I suspect she never really knew who he was herself. These portraits are obviously several hundred years old. Anyway, she wanted you to have the locket, so my job is done. Enjoy it in good health."

"I will," Nadine said, snapping the locket closed. "And thank you, Mr. Wilder."

That night Nadine lay in her bed, staring at the two tiny portraits that had shared the gold locket for nearly three centuries.

"I wonder who they were," she said to Diane, who was lying in the next bed. "What was their story? Were they brother and sister? Husband and wife? Were they lovers?"

"What I want to know is, why did Great Aunt Lucille want you to have it?" Diane said. "I mean, she didn't even know you."

"Maybe," said Nadine in a sudden burst of romanticism, "this is the key to my destiny."

She had no idea how right she was.

*   *   *

The next day, while walking to school, her new gold locket displayed proudly around her neck, Nadine had the unsettling feeling that she was being watched. Looking about, she noticed that a dark, late-model car was following her. When she turned to get a better look, she caught only a glimpse of the driver before he sped up and moved on. Although she saw the man for no more than a second or two, she knew it was the mysterious man from the funeral.

She saw the stranger again that afternoon when she was walking home. This time he appeared on the sidewalk just as she turned the corner onto Hammond Street. Startled, Nadine opened her mouth to scream. But the man remained calm and raised a hand for her to be silent.

"I'm sorry, Miss Barlow. I didn't mean to frighten you," he said in a low voice tinged with a slight eastern European accent. Nadine took a cautious step backward.

"Who are you?" she demanded, determined not to show the fear that was edging up her spine. "Why are you following me?"

"My name is Elliot Frann," the stranger replied in a soft voice. "I work for a man who very much wants to meet you."

"Who's that?" Nadine asked suspiciously.

"His name would have no meaning to you," Mr. Frann said calmly. "However, I can assure you he wishes you no harm. In fact, he has an offer for you I think you will find *very* attractive."

"Have him call my parents," Nadine said. "Now, get out of my way. I'm going home. Unless you want me to start screaming."

She stepped around Mr. Frann and prepared to move on. But as she did, the man grabbed her arm firmly. He then reached into his pocket and pulled out a gold chain from which dangled a heart-shaped gold locket.

"Look familiar?" he asked.

"That—that looks like *my* locket," Nadine said with surprise. Indeed, the locket in Mr. Frann's hand appeared to be identical to the one now hanging around her neck. She reached out to touch the locket, but Mr. Frann pulled it back teasingly.

"Look, but don't touch," Mr. Frann said, smiling. Then he began to let the locket swing slowly back and forth. Sunlight glinted off the bright gold casing. "Look carefully at the locket. Watch it move left and right, left and right. See how pretty it is. And feel your eyelids growing heavy. Heavy. Heavy . . ."

Trapped by the hypnotic rhythm of Frann's gentle voice, Nadine's eyes slowly closed and her knees buckled. The world around her turned topsy-turvy, and she found herself dropping sleepily toward the sidewalk. If she ever actually hit the concrete, she wasn't awake to feel it.

* * *

Her head still spinning, Nadine awoke some time later in what she first thought was some kind of museum. All around her were paintings, statues, and fine mahogany furniture from times long past. But as her vision cleared, she realized that this "museum" was actually the drawing room of a grand old mansion. There was a fieldstone fireplace at the far end of the room, and in it a fire was blazing.

Rising from the plush sofa she had been sleeping on, Nadine glanced out the lead-glass window and saw that night had fallen. She looked at her watch and was surprised to see that several hours had passed. It was now 9:45 P.M.

"I've got to get out of here," she mumbled, scanning the room for a door. Turning, she was startled to see a young man standing in the doorway. Tall, dark-haired, and strikingly handsome, he looked oddly familiar, even though Nadine was sure she'd never seen him before in her life. And then she realized he was a dead ringer for the young man whose picture was in her gold locket.

"My word, it *is* you," he said in awe. "For centuries I prayed for this day to come but, until now, I never really thought it possible."

"Look, I don't know who you are or what you want, and frankly I don't care," Nadine said, steadying herself against an elegant antique desk. "I just want you to take me home."

"But you *are* home, my darling Ramona," the young man said passionately. "And here we will stay for all eternity."

"This isn't my home, and my name isn't Ramona," Nadine said with rising anger. "I'm Nadine Barlow, and I live at 567 Hammond Street. If you don't let me out of here, I'm going to call the police and have you arrested for kidnapping."

"You always were a spitfire, my dear," the young man said with a smile. "Even after almost three hundred years, you're still as willful as ever."

"I'm—I'm afraid you must have me confused with someone else," said Nadine, trying to stay calm. "Now, I'm going to tell you for the last time, *take me home.*"

But Nadine's fear was growing by the second. This man obviously believed she was a three-hundred-year-old woman named Ramona, and he wasn't about to change his mind. Crazy people like him couldn't be reasoned with, and they could be very dangerous. Nadine knew that if she didn't get away from him quickly, she might never get away at all.

"All right, darling, you may leave," the young man said with a slight bow. "But first let me tell you who you are."

"I *know* who I am," Nadine stated firmly.

The young man raised a hand, signaling for Nadine to remain silent.

"You only *think* you know. But let me explain your true identity. My name is Lord Henry Bates," he said confidently as if he were teaching a history lesson. "In the year 1711 I came to America from Cornwall, England, to serve as an assistant to the Governor of His Majesty's colony of Maryland. While serving in this capacity, I met a beautiful young woman and fell deeply in love. The girl, Ramona Quigley, was only fourteen at the time, but in those days marriage at that age was not unheard of."

Nadine stared at this "Lord Bates" in disbelief. He was obviously living out some crazy historical fantasy, and she had somehow been drawn into it. Trying to appear calm and attentive, she began to glance casually about the room for something that could serve as a weapon.

"We planned to marry on Ramona's fifteenth birthday, but then she fell ill with a fever," Bates continued, his voice growing sad and distant. "Fearing she would die, I sought the help of an old woman who was rumored to be a powerful healer. She told me Ramona's life could be saved by a transfusion of vampire's blood. Of course, if the treatment was successful, I would still lose her—unless I became a vampire myself." He paused to let what he was saying sink in. "It was a heartbreaking decision," he went on solemnly, "but my love for Ramona was so strong that I was willing to sacrifice my own immortal soul to spend eternity with her. And so I arranged for both Ramona and myself to become members of the undead."

Nadine's eyes now came to rest on Bates, whose sadness and pain seemed uncomfortably real. Despite herself, she was actually beginning to feel sorry for this tortured man. Not only that, but somehow she was beginning to sense that his story, as farfetched as it sounded, could be the truth.

"So, what you're telling me is that you and Ramona actually became vampires?" Nadine asked, afraid of his answer.

Bates sighed painfully. "Unfortunately, no. The dual transfusion took place precisely at midnight as the old witch had instructed," he said. "But something went wrong. While I smoothly made the transition from mortal to vampire, my dear Ramona died instantly. Perhaps she was already too far gone and the shock of the transfusion was too great." He shook his head. "I'll never really know. But one thing I did know was that I couldn't live without her. And now that I could never die, I wouldn't even join her in death! I was doomed to walk the earth alone for all eternity."

Bates stepped closer to Nadine, looked deep into her eyes, then took the locket at her throat in his hand and held it gently.

"This locket—the symbol of our undying love—was given to her younger sister who, in turn, passed it down to her daughter years later," Bates explained. "I have followed its progress over the centuries in the belief—the *hope*—that its power would someday bring my dearest Ramona back to me. And now, at long last, I see that it has."

He stared into Nadine's eyes with a look so powerful that she nearly fainted.

"You—you think *I'm* Ramona?" she managed to stammer. "But—but I'm *not!*"

"I know that you are," he said. "I can see it in your eyes, and I can feel it in my soul. Look deep into your heart, and you will know I speak the truth."

In fact, Nadine was feeling a strong, almost overwhelming attraction to this man. But her rational mind continued to insist that both he and this situation were totally insane.

"Now that I've found you, I will never lose you again," Bates went on, his voice powerful. "The time has come for you to join me in immortality!"

He opened his mouth to reveal two long fangs. His eyes blazed red as he lowered his mouth toward Nadine's neck.

"No!" Nadine screamed, somehow managing to break away from Bates and run. She sprinted toward the door, but he suddenly appeared in front of her and grabbed her by the arm.

"You're mine, Ramona!" he bellowed. "And I am yours, forever and for all time!"

Again his fangs came down swiftly toward her neck, but at the same time, she raised her foot and slammed it forcefully into the vampire's kneecap. Bates gave a painful howl and lost his grip on her arm. Grabbing a nearby ceramic vase, Nadine swung it into Bates' chest.

The blow took the vampire by surprise, and the impact sent him stumbling backward into the roaring fire in the huge stone fireplace.

"Ramona! *Noooo!*" Bates screamed as flames danced around him.

Looking on in horror, Nadine watched as the vampire thrashed about madly for several moments, then vanished, leaving no sign that there had ever been a Lord Henry Bates. Not even ashes.

"You have killed my master," came a voice from behind her. Nadine spun around to find Elliot Frann standing in the doorway. She gasped in fear. What would he do to her? Kill her?

"I don't know how to thank you," Frann said. "Bates held me in his power and forced me to do his bidding for these last fifteen years. Thanks to you, I'm free at last. If there's anything I can do—"

"Take me home," Nadine said immediately. "I'll tell my folks I went to the library and fell asleep. No one has to know about any of this."

* * *

Weeks later, after much searching, Nadine located an old book on American colonial history at the town library. It indicated that a man named Lord Henry Bates had served in the government of colonial Maryland in the early eighteenth century. So, at least that much of Bates' story had been true. But, much to her disappointment, there was no mention of what happened to him after that.

Nadine continued to wear the heart-shaped locket containing the pictures of Bates and his love, Ramona. As time passed, she became more and more convinced that

Bates' story had been true, and that she was the reincarnation of this dead girl's spirit. She began to wonder if she and Bates could have made a life together. She even daydreamed about what life would have been like as a vampire.

This thought was on her mind when, two years later, she attended the funeral of her uncle Albert, who had died following a long illness. She and her parents were returning to their car when she noticed a man staring at them from a row of nearby headstones. Like most of the mourners, he was dressed in dark clothes. He also wore a dark blue scarf over his face, even though the temperature was well above 50 degrees. Looking at the man, Nadine believed she saw the reason for the scarf: his face looked scarred and blistered, as if he had survived a horrendous fire.

Continuing to study the man, Nadine fixed on his eyes. They looked uncomfortably familiar. Nadine gasped suddenly as recognition dawned.

Deep, dark, and filled with longing, the eyes staring back at her belonged to Lord Henry Bates.

The Vampyr Hunter's Apprentice

A t age ten, all the young men in the English village of Brianswood who were not already engaged in farming were required to apprentice to one of the local craftsmen. One could learn to master the blacksmith's anvil, the cooper's hammer, or the tailor's needle. Apprenticing to the cobbler meant spending eight to ten years learning the craft of making shoes, while working for the mason meant years spent perfecting the exacting art of stonework and bricklaying.

These were all noble and honorable professions, yet young Timothy Horn wanted none of them. Ever since Tim was five, he had wanted to be a knight and to battle the enemies of his country. The warm days of summer would find young Timothy dashing about the grassy hills on the outskirts of Brianswood. Brandishing his wooden sword and tin shield, Timothy engaged in mortal combat with evil knights, fire-breathing dragons, and armored demons that existed only in his youthful imagination.

Timothy's mother did all she could to discourage her son's strange ideas. After all, in thirteenth-century England, knighthood was a privilege reserved only for those born of noble blood. During times of war, commoners like Tim were merely sacrificial lambs to be marched ahead of the mounted knights, armed with only a crude sword or mace to catch the first volley of the enemy's arrows or the slash of their swords. At best, a boy like Tim could hope to serve as a knight's squire, tending to his horse, polishing his armor, and sharpening his weapons. But to become a knight himself? That was an impossible dream.

So, on his tenth birthday, at his mother's insistence, Timothy agreed to apprentice to his uncle, the town bootmaker. But Timothy showed little talent for laces and leatherwork and was rejected after only four months. His mother then convinced her cousin, a respected carpenter, to take the boy under his wing. This position lasted only two months, ending abruptly when Tim accidentally drove a two-inch nail through his master's left index finger.

For the next two years Timothy jumped from job to job, working at times for a butcher, a baker, and, yes, even a candlestick maker. But all of these attempts inevitably ended in disaster.

By the time Tim was thirteen, his mother—who had raised the boy alone since his father's death a decade earlier—had come to her wit's end. Her son appeared unsuited for virtually every job in the village, and he now had a reputation for being lazy and stubborn. This could prove disastrous, for in medieval England, a young man without a trade was worse than worthless—

he was viewed as a drain on society, a parasite to be driven out with the rats and other vermin. Whether he liked it or not, Timothy would have to find a steady job or live in shame outside his native town.

"But I *know* what I want to do," Timothy insisted upon hearing his mother's ultimatum. "I want to be a knight and fight for the king."

"And you know that's impossible," his mother said, barely able to control her rising anger. "You haven't the breeding for it."

"But I'm better with a sword than most men *twice* my age!" Timothy insisted. "I can handle the broadsword and the sabre. What's more, I've skill with the mace and the crossbow as well." His chest swelled with pride. "There's no better fighter in all of Brianswood!"

To prove his point, he picked up a knife sitting on the kitchen table, turned, and flung it underhanded toward the wall twenty feet away. The knife found its target, a knothole no more than an inch wide, and sank its point nearly two inches into the wood.

"All true, my son. You do, indeed, have the skills of a true warrior," his mother agreed. "But you cannot change the laws of nature. You were born a commoner, not a nobleman. And you must choose a commoner's occupation. Like it or not, there is no other way."

It was at this time that fate revealed itself in the form of a mysterious stranger who rode into Brianswood under the light of a full moon. Dressed in black leather and trailing a black satin cape, this ghostly figure found lodging at a local inn and from there began asking questions of the townsfolk. Word soon spread that this stranger, who went by the name of Thomas

Blackthorne, was a demon hunter, and had come to Brianswood in pursuit of a powerful vampyr who was terrorizing the English countryside.

As soon as Timothy Horn heard of Blackthorne and his mission, the young man realized that he had found his destiny. He immediately ran to the inn where the vampyr hunter was staying and offered himself as an apprentice.

"You seem like a sincere young lad," said Blackthorne, his bright blue eyes sparkling behind a face laced with the scars of countless battles with evildoers. "But I travel alone. I always have. Sorry, boy, but I have no use for an apprentice."

"But surely you can use a boy to feed and groom your horse, ready your weapons, and mend your armor," Timothy persisted.

"I've done well enough on my own these past twenty years," Blackthorne said, stroking his coarse black beard.

"Then consider this, good sir," Timothy said, still brimming with confidence. "The day will come when you will no longer be able to fight evil in this world. Who will carry on the battle then? Who will protect the good people of England from the scourge of the undead? Train me and you not only gain a valuable ally today, but you guarantee that the victories you claim in the present will not be lost in the years ahead."

Again Blackthorne stroked his beard, then took a swallow of warm ale from the large clay stein before him. Wiping its froth from his lips with the back of his massive hand, he looked back toward Timothy and nodded.

"You speak well for such a young lad," the old vampyr hunter said. "And your point is well taken. Perhaps I *should* train an apprentice to take my place when I am no longer able to carry on the fight. But, still, the question remains, why you?"

"Because I am pure of heart and strong of spirit," Timothy replied. "My head is clear, my body is strong, and I can handle a sword as well as any man." He paused and thought for a moment. "And I have no fear of danger."

"The man who says he does not fear danger is either a liar or a fool," Blackthorne said gruffly. "And as to your martial skills . . ."

In a flash Blackthorne pulled a dagger out from a sheath hidden beneath his tunic and sent its point plunging toward young Timothy's heart. Just as quickly Tim blocked the hunter's downward thrust with his left forearm, grabbed the man's right hand with his own, and pressing a pressure point just above the base of Blackthorne's thumb, managed to free the knife from the older man's grasp.

As the knife clattered to the floor, Blackthorne turned to Tim with an expression of delighted astonishment.

"Perhaps you can be of service to me after all," the vampyr hunter said pleasantly. "I'm pursuing an elusive vampyr named Ian Shades. He's killed over two dozen people from here to the eastern coast. I've just received word of his possible whereabouts and need to leave as soon as possible to confront him. Meet me here tomorrow at dawn."

"Yes, sir!" Timothy said eagerly. "You won't live to regret this!"

Timothy ran straight home and told his mother the great news. Hearing that her one and only son was about to apprentice to a vampyr hunter, she fell onto a chair and clutched at her heart in despair.

"This demon has come to snatch you away from me," she moaned. "Oh, Timothy, stay! He's sure to corrupt your soul."

"No, Mother, you don't understand," Timothy said, gently taking his mother's quivering hand in his own. "We are doing good work. Together, we will vanquish these undead creatures who have brought misery upon our land."

"No!" his mother cried sharply. "You will mention this matter no more! I forbid it! Even to speak of such things will bring a curse upon this house and all of those within it!"

Timothy lowered his head in silence. There was no use trying to convince his mother that his cause was just. Like so many of the people in Brianswood, she was intensely superstitious. She believed that speaking of demons would attract them and staying silent would keep them away. But Timothy knew better. He knew that evil was a force that could not be ignored. It had to be faced head-on.

So, late that night Timothy gathered his few personal possessions in a brown cloth sack. He left his house in the early morning hours and ran to the inn to meet Thomas Blackthorne at sunrise. Then, as the first rays of dawn cast their glow over the horizon, he hurried along on foot while the vampyr hunter rode forth toward his rendezvous with Ian Shades.

For the next two weeks Blackthorne traveled across

the English countryside, through dense forests, across grassy meadows, through frigid rivers, and over fog-shrouded moors. Timothy followed him obediently. At night Blackthorne gave him lessons in the art of hunting vampyrs. He taught him how vampyrs are born of corrupted blood, how they get their superhuman strength by absorbing the souls of the living, and how they can travel by night as bats, wolves, or even mist. He revealed how vampyrs can be repelled by garlic, roses, or silvered glass. He also told Timothy that vampyrs could be killed only by fire, sunlight, or a wooden stake driven straight through their black hearts.

These sessions also featured intense training in the art of hand-to-hand combat. Blackthorne put Timothy through an endless series of painful exercises designed to build his muscles, heighten his reflexes, and hone his tactical thinking. Although always driven to his physical limits, often frustrated and frequently humiliated, Timothy never once complained about this routine. For he was committed to being a vampyr slayer at any and all costs.

On the fifteenth day of their journey, Timothy and Blackthorne came in sight of a black stone fortress standing on the edge of a mist-shrouded swamp. The sky was densely overcast, making it virtually impossible to make out any details beyond the huge, dark mass of the castle itself.

"This is it," Blackthorne said in a voice suddenly gripped with tension. "Before you stands the lair of Ian Shades."

"Is he in there?" Timothy asked anxiously. "Is he in there right now?"

Blackthorne nodded solemnly. "I can feel him. I can feel his coldness." He turned to Timothy. "The vampyr's dark soul is like a vast, bottomless pit that sucks up all the light for miles around. Just look at the sky."

Timothy looked up at the dark clouds that blocked out any trace of the sun, making it impossible to determine the time of day. "Do we wait until nighttime to attack?" he asked.

"No, we attack *now*," Blackthorne said, mounting his horse. "The night only feeds his powers. He's most vulnerable now, in the daylight."

Without another word, Blackthorne spurred his horse forward across the moor. Timothy ran after him, a sour ache deep in the pit of his stomach. For the first time, evil was not just an idea. It was *real*, and within minutes, he would confront it face-to-face.

When they arrived at the base of the mammoth black stone fortress, they could see no entrance except a single twenty-foot-high wooden gate. Locked with a steel bar, it looked impenetrable.

"We'll have to scale the walls," Blackthorne said, removing a grappling hook and a length of sturdy rope from his saddlebag. He gave them both to Timothy. "Go to it, boy."

Realizing what he was expected to do, Timothy twirled the heavy hook over his head several times, then let it fly toward the battlements along the upper edge of the castle walls. His first attempt failed, but on his second the hook found a secure roost on a parapet.

Blackthorne climbed first, moving hand over hand, his feet planted firmly against the fortress's rough stone walls. Timothy followed close behind, huffing and puffing as he struggled to pull himself and his heavy equipment up what was at least a forty-foot vertical climb.

Arriving at the top of the wall just seconds behind his master, Timothy was relieved to find the area deserted. He freed the grappling hook, wound up the rope, and stowed both in the bulky leather sack in which he carried most of their vampyr-hunting gear.

"Which way now?" he asked.

"We must locate the keep," Blackthorne stated, referring to the vaultlike chamber that lay at the heart of virtually all European castles. "It is the most secure area of the fortress and therefore the most likely place for the vampyr to 'keep' his coffin." He grinned. "Come, my boy. We've a vampyr to awaken."

After several minutes they located an entrance to the castle proper and began a slow, steady descent down a narrow spiral staircase. To Timothy it was like a twisted plunge into another world. Blackthorne had been right—the place was *cold*. But it wasn't the kind of cold that came with the snows of winter. No, this was a deeper, more disturbing cold. It reached down into your soul and threatened to tear the life force from your very being. And with every step he took, the stronger this dreadful feeling grew inside of Timothy.

Finding themselves in a brick-lined corridor devoid of natural sunlight, Blackthorne and Timothy lit torches. They then proceeded slowly through a maze of interconnecting passageways toward the castle's keep. Guided by instincts sharpened by years of experience, Blackthorne located the chamber within minutes. It was cube-shaped, forty feet long on each side, and just as tall. There was only one way in or out—the doorway in which they now stood. Timothy's eyes widened at what lay in the center of the chamber. It was a six-and-a-half-foot-long stone sarcophagus covered with some kind of ancient carvings.

"There," Blackthorne intoned softly. "That is where Ian sleeps. And that is where he will meet his death. Come, we must move quickly."

Timothy followed Blackthorne into the keep, then set his equipment bag beside the intricately carved coffin. The old vampyr hunter carefully removed a stake and hammer from the bag, got himself into position, and gave Timothy a silent nod.

With all his strength, Timothy pushed against the heavy stone cover. It made a low, grinding noise, then slowly slid to one side. The rancid smell of death rose from the coffin. Blackthorne leaned forward, raised his hammer to strike—then stopped. The coffin was empty.

"Oh, no," Timothy groaned. "We're too late. He must have fled."

"No," Blackthorne said, looking quickly about. "He's here . . . and he's close. I can feel him."

"Right you are, old friend!" a voice boomed above them, amplified by the hard stone walls. "Welcome to my humble home."

Timothy raised his flaming torch, looked straight up, and couldn't believe his eyes. A man dressed in dark, noble robes was floating forty feet above them, just inches from the ceiling!

"Shades!" Blackthorne bellowed. "Come down here and face me like a man!"

"But I'm not a man," Shades replied with a grin. "Oh, no, Blackthorne, I am much, *much* more."

And then Ian Shades seemed to simply vanish. In his place, a large brown bat appeared, its leathery wings beating frantically. With an ear-piercing shriek, the creature dived toward them, its fangs aimed at Blackthorne's neck.

With lightning speed, Blackthorne dropped the stake, whipped out a sword, and slashed at the bat as it winged through the air. Stunned, the beast fell to the ground, an entire chunk of its wing sheared off.

"Now!" Timothy shouted. "Kill it!"

"We must be cautious," Blackthorne warned, slowly retrieving the wooden stake. "Shades is filled with all sorts of mischief."

Blackthorne advanced cautiously toward the bat, which was now huddled on the stone floor in a shivering ball. Taking a deep breath, he gripped the stake in both hands and prepared to stab it through the creature's body. But just as Blackthorne raised the stake over his head, a startling transformation occurred. What had been a wounded bat suddenly became a ferocious wolf. Its eyes blazing red, the wolf snarled and leaped for Blackthorne's throat. The creature knocked the stake from the vampyr slayer's hand and sent him sprawling to the floor.

In an instant the wolf was on Blackthorne's chest. It took all his strength to hold the beast's snarling mouth away from his pulsing jugular vein.

"Run!" Blackthorne screamed. "Run, boy! Run while you still can!"

But Timothy would not leave his master to die. Instead, he dashed across the room to where the wooden stake now lay. Holding his blazing torch in his left hand, the brave apprentice picked the stake up with his right and turned toward the vicious canine. "Shades!" he screamed.

The wolf turned toward Timothy and roared with murderous rage. Then, without warning, it leaped for the boy.

Instantly Timothy threw the stake underhanded, just as he had done with the knife in his own home two weeks earlier. The stake found its target, the center of the wolf's heart. As the weapon pierced its skin, the beast shrieked in agony. When the wolf hit the floor, it returned to the form of Ian Shades.

"But . . . you're just a boy," Shades gasped, trying to remove the stake from his blood-soaked chest.

"Not any more," Blackthorne said, rising to his feet. "Today he became a vampyr killer."

Still filled with disbelief, Shades' eyes turned to Timothy Horn . . . then closed forever. Moments later, what had been a bat, a wolf, and a vampyr was now nothing but a pile of gray ash.

"You show some promise after all," Blackthorne said, gripping Tim's shoulder firmly. "But don't think too much of yourself. Your education has just begun. You still have much to learn."

"Yes, sir," said Timothy, and he began to dutifully gather up their tools and weapons. Blackthorne had said he was a vampyr killer. Now Tim wanted to learn every aspect of the art, from hunting and tracking to slaying the bloodthirsty creatures. Closing up the leather bag, he caught Blackthorne looking his way, a glint of pride in the old man's eyes. *Yes,* Timothy thought, *I have truly found my destiny.*

"Come, lad, it's time to ride," Blackthorne said as he led Timothy to the doorway. "I've word of another vampyr who has made his home on the river Thames in a small town called London."

"I'm with you, sir," Timothy said.

As they left the deathly cold keep, Blackthorne rubbed the bloody scratch on his hand, the one that Ian Shades had given him as they struggled. Had Tim looked back, he may have noticed the strange way Blackthorne stared at him. Maybe then Timothy Horn would have known that his next encounter with a vampyr would be sooner than he thought.

Q & A

Q: All right, is this thing running?
A: Yes, David, I believe it is.
Q: Testing, testing, one-two-three . . .
A: I said, it's working. See, the little red light is on.
Q: Okay, great. Let's see . . . This is David Grant. The date is November twenty-fourth. It's eight o'clock at night. And for my year-end science project, I'm doing research on vampires—
A: Please, David, do not use that word.
Q: What word?
A: "Vampire."
Q: But that's what you are.
A: It is an antiquated term. And rather offensive. It makes us sound, well, evil. Believe me, we are not evil. We're merely beings who follow our own nature.
Q: Sorry. What would you like to be called? "Undead?" "Nosferatu?"
A: Actually, we prefer "differently animated."

Q: That makes you sound like some kind of cartoon character.

A: Check your dictionary. The formal definition of "animation" is "the quality or condition of being alive, active, spirited, or vigorous." As our name implies, we are indeed animated, only in a way different from yourself and your kind.

Q: Makes sense to me. Uh, let's get started, okay?

A: Go straight for the jugular.

Q: Huh?

A: That's our way of saying, "Go for it."

Q: Uh, right . . . Now, as we agreed when you responded to my ad, I won't use your real name in my report to protect your privacy. So, what should I call you?

A: I always liked the name Tyrone. How about that?

Q: Sure . . . Tyrone. Now, let's begin with a simple question. How old are you?

A: Well, since we differently animated don't age, perhaps a more relevant question would be, in what year was I born? The answer to that is 1865.

Q: Cool. That's the year the American Civil War ended. Did you know Abraham Lincoln?

A: How could I? I was an infant when he was killed.

Q: Right. Did you know any other famous people? You know, like Teddy Roosevelt?

A: No.

Q: Babe Ruth?

A: No.

Q: John Wayne?

A: Actually, I never met any celebrities. We tend to be very private people. And, to tell you the truth, we're not particularly fond of how we've been depicted by Hollywood. We're not really monsters, you know.

Q: I'm only thirteen. That's kind of out of my hands.

A: Yes, I suppose so.

Q: So, anyway, where were you born?

A: Springfield, Missouri.

Q: You're kidding.

A: Why would I "kid"?

Q: I don't know. That just seems so, you know . . . *ordinary*.

A: We're not all from Transylvania, you know. Quite the contrary. You'll find that the differently animated come from all parts of the world and from all walks of life. We're policemen, insurance salesmen, lawyers . . .

Q: My dad's a lawyer.

A: You might want to check the date on his birth certificate.

Q: My dad's not a vampire—I mean, differently animated.

A: Sorry. I didn't mean to imply—

Q: Forget it. Just tell me how you became, uh, what you are.

A: It was the year 1904. I was thirty-nine years old at the time, and I had traveled to St. Louis to visit the World's Fair. While staying at a boardinghouse on the city's South Side, I met an attractive young lady by the name of Emily Dunsworthy. She was an assistant to the Great Garibaldi, a knife-thrower. It was her job to be strapped to a spinning wheel and have knives thrown at her.

Q: Ouch! What if he hit her?

A: Ah, that was the beauty of it. Emily was a vampire.

Q: But I thought you said not to use that word.

A: I said for *you* not to use it. And I'm only using it because, back then, it was the accepted term. Anyway, the point is, Garibaldi's knives couldn't kill her. After all, he wasn't throwing wooden stakes.

Q: Tell me how she turned you into a vampire.

A: Well, it was quite frightening, actually.

Q: Tell me.

A: You're certain you can handle it?

Q: Hey, once me and my family were driving through the mountains and my kid brother got carsick and threw up in my lap. If I could take that, I can take anything.

A: Very well. Here's what happened. I was quite fond of Emily, and I frequently went to the fair just to watch her show. One night, after her last performance, she coaxed me into accompanying her on a walk around the fairgrounds. Everything was closed, but there were a few maintenance workers milling about, so she got one of them to start up the Tunnel of Love ride for us. Well, when we entered that first tunnel, I took Emily in my arms and prepared to kiss her—but she bit my neck instead.

Q: She gave you a hickey?

A: Believe me, David, this was no mere hickey. Her bite drew blood. My blood. She drank from my veins as if she were drinking wine from a goblet.

Q: Did it hurt?

A: Actually, after her initial bite, I found the experience to be, well, quite remarkable.

Q: How so?

A: Well, although she nearly drained all my blood,

she didn't take enough to kill me, and I felt a new . . . a *different* life entering my body. Anyway, I was pretty dazed and weakened by the whole experience, but somehow I managed to make it back to the boarding-house.

After that, I slept for nearly twenty-four hours. When I awoke, I discovered that I could no longer tolerate sunlight or eat normal foods. I wanted blood. That's when Emily taught me how to feed—off the living.

Q: You mean, you *killed* people?

A: Well, not exactly.

Q: Then how?

A: I got my nourishment from animals. Stray dogs and cats, mostly. Now and then I'd spring for a live pig. For Thanksgiving, I drank a turkey—

Q: But you're a vamp—I mean . . . Well, I thought your kind were supposed to kill *people*.

A: Some of us do. Personally, I like people. They're good for conversation. They make me laugh. Why kill something you like?

Q: You mean, you've never killed *anyone*?

A: Well, actually, there was this one fellow . . .

Q: Yes?

A: I was living in Chicago. It was right after a huge blizzard, in the dead of winter. I'd spent almost two hours clearing myself a parking space on the street when some guy just took the space right out from under me.

Q: So you killed him?

A: I'd say he deserved it, wouldn't you?

Q: Uh, let's move on. Are you rich? In the movies, vampires are always rich. You know, they live in big castles and wear tuxedos and—

A: Let me ask you something, kid. Do you know what it's like being able to take only night jobs?

Q: I don't have a job.

A: There aren't a lot of choices out there. Night watchman. Newspaper delivery man. Convenience store clerk. None of them will make you rich, believe me.

Q: So you're not rich.

A: I do okay. I've made some good investments. Hey, you put ten dollars a week in the bank for a hundred years, the interest adds up.

Q: Let's talk about myths about the differently animated. Is it true you don't reflect in mirrors?

A: True, and it makes shaving in the morning a real bear. That and combing your hair. Ever try to make a straight part with no reflection to guide you? Well, let me tell you, it's not easy.

Q: How about ways to *kill* a vampire?

A: I told you not to call me that. Besides, that's a subject I'd rather not discuss.

Q: Aw, come on . . .

A: How about we talk about ways to kill humans? Does that sound like fun to you? Let's talk about poisons and guns and knives and strangling and burning people at the stake . . . oh, I *do* hate that word.

Q: All right, all right. I get your point.

A: Show some sensitivity, would you?

Q: All right. Just a few more questions. Tell me, uh, Tyrone, what is it like to be able to live forever?

A: Let me tell you something, David. Immortality is no picnic. After the first hundred years, it gets awfully boring. Music, art, movies, television, they all seem to settle into a bland sameness after a while. In fact, there are times when, well, I just want to end it all.

Q: Then why don't you?

A: It's almost impossible for one of my kind to take his own life. But . . . someone like you could help me.

Q: Whoa. You're not asking me to—

A: Put me out of my misery? Yes, I suppose I am.

Q: You're crazy. I could never kill anyone, not even a vampire!

A: There, you see how you put that? "Not even a vampire." You could just as easily have said, "Not even a loathsome creature like you." And you're right. I really *am* loathsome. So kill me now—or I'll turn you into one of *me*!

Q: You wouldn't.

A: Try me. Now, here's a stake and a mallet. I'll lie down, and you put the point of the stake right here over my heart.

Q: Like this?

A: A little higher and to the left.

Q: Here?

A: Perfect.

Q: Now what?

A: Hammer it into my chest.

Q: I don't think I can . . .

A: I said, *do it*!

Q: Will there be blood?

A: What do you care? Technically, it's not my blood anyway.

Q: All right. Here goes. Ugh!

A: Ouch! Oh, come on, David. You're stronger than that. You didn't even break the skin. Now, hit me again—like your life depended on it.

Q: Well, here goes nothing. Ugh!!!

A: Ahhhhhhhh!!!!

Q: Oh, jeez! What a mess! When Mom sees this, she's going to kill me!

(Knock, knock, knock)

?: Hey, what's going on in there?

Q: Huh? Who's there?

?: I'm a friend of Ben's. Hey, what is this? All this blood! What did you do to Ben!? You . . . you *killed* him!

Q: He told me to kill him, I swear!

?: Who are you?

Q: I'm David Grant. I'm doing a school project on vampires. I put an ad in the paper asking for real-life vampires to interview, and he answered.

?: So, he told you all about himself?

Q: Yeah. And at the end, he forced me to kill him. He said he was tired of immortality.

?: The coward! I should have known he'd resort to something like this. Ben never had the stomach for our kind of existence.

Q: "Our kind?" You mean, you're . . . ?

?: Since 1833.

Q: Wow. Cool! You ever kill people?

?: All the time.

Q: Oh.

?: People just like you.

Q: That's very interesting, but I really should be going.

?: No, no. Stay awhile. Please. The evening is still young. You wanted to learn about vampires? I can show you everything you ever wanted to know.

Q: Uh, thanks, but I really have quite enough for my report . . . .

?: I insist.

Q: No, please. Get away from the door.

?: We'll just turn this machine off . . .

Q: Stay away from me or I'll hit you with this hammer!

?: Give that to me now . . . Ow! My arm! Come back here, you worthless human! Come back and I'll teach you something about vampires! Something you can take to your grave!

(End of recording)

The Strange Case of Amanda Talbot

—

manda Talbot was Westmont Junior High's biggest hypochondriac. Listening to Amanda talk, you'd think she'd never had a healthy day in her life. If she wasn't complaining about a headache, runny nose, or sore muscle, she was suffering from allergies, asthma, or stomach cramps.

Amanda's talent for attracting disease was uncanny. When someone at Westmont became sick, Amanda would have the same illness by the end of the day. Whenever the TV news reported an outbreak of flu, you could count on Amanda to be in bed with a fever before the next commercial. Once she actually claimed to have strep throat, appendicitis, chicken pox, and food poisoning all at the same time.

Of course, Amanda didn't limit herself to common illnesses. Once she believed she was suffering from malaria, a disease common to the tropics and carried by mosquitoes. (This was in Des Moines, Iowa, in the dead of winter.) Another time Amanda was convinced she was the victim of a rare African parasite that causes a person's legs to swell to three times their normal size. This was despite the fact that her legs had never swelled and that she'd never been anywhere near Africa.

None of these conditions ever proved fatal, or even long lasting. Amanda was usually up and about within a day or so, ready to catch the next epidemic she heard about in the hallways or read about in the newspaper.

By the time she entered the eighth grade, Amanda had contracted more diseases—mostly imagined—than most people get in their entire lifetime. Despite her tendency to become "deathly ill" at a moment's notice, Amanda always managed to be well when it came time for Myra Lieberman's annual Halloween party.

For as long as anyone could remember, the Liebermans had given the absolute best Halloween parties in town. The food was great. The music was sensational. And the Liebermans gave terrific prizes for kids wearing the best costumes. Anyone who was anyone at Westmont Junior High was invited, and not accepting an invitation was a sure way to be labeled a loser.

Amanda had never won a prize at the Liebermans', but this year she was sure she would. She was going as Marie Antoinette, the eighteenth-century French queen who was beheaded in 1793 during the French Revolution. Practically from the moment she failed to win a prize at last year's party, Amanda had started work on her costume. She chose the fabrics and other materials and sewed away when she wasn't in bed or visiting doctors.

Amanda's mother had taught her how to use a sewing machine when she was still in grade school, and now she could play the device like a fine instrument. After months of drawing, cutting, sewing, and stitching, she had created a colorful eighteenth-century-style evening gown so authentic that it would have been the envy of a Hollywood costumer. Topped off with a tall white wig and her mother's costume jewelry, the dress was literally fit for a queen.

Finally Halloween arrived. Amanda was dressed and ready to go by six o'clock, a full hour before the party was scheduled to begin. She spent the remaining time in bed, building up her strength, until finally her father announced it was time to leave. Together, they drove the mile and a half to the Liebermans' handsome two-story home. The street was already buzzing with young monsters, aliens, knights, commandos, Egyptian princesses, and every other conceivable character.

Amanda's entrance at the Liebermans' was as grand as her costume. All the other kids stopped to stare and whisper as the magnificent monarch strode regally through the front door, her head held high, her nose even higher.

"Amanda? Is that *you*?" gasped Cybil Stevens, a long-time classmate who was dressed as a boring old nurse.

"It's me!" Amanda said gleefully, waving her jeweled fan as though she was royalty.

"What an incredible costume!" Cybil gushed, reaching out to touch the fabric. "Did you rent it? You couldn't possibly have made it yourself!"

"But I did!" Amanda announced proudly. "Besides,

rented costumes don't qualify for prizes."

Just then, Myra Lieberman and Bonnie Stone rushed over. "You look fantastic!" Myra screamed. She was dressed as a blood-covered zombie. "You'll win a prize, for sure!"

"Absolutely!" cried Bonnie, who had come wearing her old basketball jersey and a ripped pair of sweat-pants. "That's the most realistic costume I've ever seen!"

Suddenly the life of the party, Amanda loved all the attention she was getting. Gone were her usual concerns about airborne germs, contaminated food, and unsanitized serving dishes. Instead, she flirted with all the boys who now were paying attention to her—Amanda Talbot, Westmont Junior High's former Miss Nobody.

In fact, when Mrs. Lieberman announced a dance contest, half the guys clamored to have Amanda as their partner. She was about to choose Tom Dayton, a very cute jock who'd come dressed as King Tut, when another, older boy stepped forward and offered his hand.

"Amanda is dancing with me," he declared as he bent down to kiss her gloved hand.

Who is this guy? Amanda thought, her heart fluttering. *I don't recognize him from anywhere.*

Tall and *very* good looking, with high cheekbones and flashing blue eyes, the young man escorting Amanda onto the dance floor was dressed as Count Dracula. His costume was elegant, complete with tuxedo shirt, silk-lined cape, and jeweled medallion. "Madame," he said, taking her gloved hand in his.

"Sir," Amanda answered, her blood rushing to her face.

At first Amanda found it difficult to move in her heavy, multilayered dress. Her partner's movements were so strong and fluid, however, that she found she had only to sway with the music. She looked like a professional dancer in a music video. After the first song, the music switched to a ballad. The "count," as he liked to be called, clasped his hands around Amanda's waist and they began to slow dance.

"You dance divinely, Your Highness," he said in what sounded to Amanda like a fake eastern European accent.

"Why, *merci, mon Count,*" Amanda replied in her best French accent. "Are you a relative of the Liebermans?"

"Why, whatever gave you that idea?" he asked.

"I don't recognize you from school," Amanda replied, batting her eyelashes. "So I thought maybe you were a cousin or something."

The young man laughed.

"No, Amanda. I am merely a . . . guest," he said mysteriously.

"So, you're a friend?" Amanda asked.

"I would certainly like to be yours," he said with a smile.

Amanda blushed. This young man was positively charming, certainly more so than the immature nerds and jocks at school.

"You know, all this dancing has made me thirsty," Amanda said, looking deeply into her partner's eyes. "Would you like some punch?"

"Thank you," the young man said with a tight smile. "I am thirsty, too, but I do not drink . . . punch."

Just then, the lights went out and the music went silent. Immediately the party dissolved into chaos.

"Hey, who turned out the lights?" a boy called.

"Ouch! Get off my foot!" a girl cried nearby.

Confused, Amanda was turning about, trying to get her bearings, when she felt a sting on the side of her neck. She instinctively slapped at it and felt something warm and sticky on her fingertips.

A moment later the lights snapped back on and the music started up again.

"Must've been a momentary blackout," Mr. Lieberman announced, standing near the stereo. "We may have blown a fuse between all the lights and the stereo—"

Suddenly Mr. Lieberman's sentence was interrupted by a high-pitched scream. Everyone turned toward Amanda. She was standing alone in the center of the living room, staring at blood dripping from her fingertips.

Mrs. Lieberman rushed Amanda to the bathroom, where they found an inch-long scratch on the side of Amanda's neck. Mrs. Lieberman quickly treated it with an antibiotic cream and then put an adhesive bandage over the wound.

"How did you get that?" she asked Amanda as she secured the bandage in place.

"I don't know. It happened during the blackout," Amanda replied. "I was dancing with the guy dressed as a vampire. Maybe he knows."

"Vampire?" asked Mrs. Lieberman. "I don't recall letting in anyone dressed like that."

"He said he was your guest," Amanda explained. "He never told me his name."

Mrs. Lieberman turned to her husband, who was standing in the bathroom doorway. He shrugged in ignorance.

"I saw a Frankenstein monster, two werewolves, and a couple of zombies out there, but no vampires," he reported.

"I'll show you," Amanda said, annoyed, and marched back into the living room to find her tall, dark suitor. But he was nowhere to be seen. Increasingly upset, Amanda stomped through the kitchen, the dining room, and then into each of the home's bedrooms. There was no sign of the handsome young "count" with the fake Transylvanian accent.

"Did you see the vampire I was dancing with?" she asked Cybil Stevens.

"Who?" Cybil responded blankly.

"The *vampire*," Amanda repeated. "We were dancing together just before the blackout."

"I was in the kitchen," Cybil said. "I didn't see any vampire."

Amanda stared at her friend. She couldn't believe what she was hearing. How could she not have noticed such a hunk!

She was ready to search the attic if she had to when a wave of dizziness swept over Amanda and she was forced to take a seat on the couch.

"Are you all right, honey?" asked Mrs. Lieberman with concern.

"She's probably overheated in that heavy costume," Mr. Lieberman remarked. "I'll get her a glass of water."

As Mr. Lieberman left, Amanda's mind whirled with questions. What if the boy she had danced with wasn't a guest at all? What if he wasn't just *dressed* like a vampire but really *was* a vampire? That would mean she had just been bitten by one of the undead! And because she had been left alive, she was doomed to become a bloodsucker herself!

"Here you go, Amanda," Mr. Lieberman said, returning with a glass of ice-cold water.

"No," Amanda gasped, knocking the glass out of her host's hand. "I-I've got to go home. Please call my dad. I can't stay here!"

"But what about the costume contest?" Mrs. Lieberman asked. "You're dressed so beautifully. Why don't you stay a while longer?"

"*I have to go home before it's too late!*" Amanda screamed.

The Liebermans stared at Amanda in shock.

"I'll call your father, dear," Mrs. Lieberman said in a calm voice. "Now, just relax."

Amanda's father arrived fifteen minutes later to find his daughter sitting at the kitchen table, looking as white as a sheet.

"All right, what's wrong this time?" he asked. "Salmonella? Ptomaine poisoning? Botulism?"

"She was scratched on the neck during a brief electrical blackout we had," Mr. Lieberman explained.

"I wasn't scratched, I was *bitten*," Amanda insisted. "I was bitten by a vampire, and now I'm going to be one, too!"

"All right, Amanda, let's go home," her father said sternly. He turned and whispered to the Liebermans. "If it's not one thing with her, it's another. Don't worry. She'll be over it by morning."

But Amanda wasn't over "it" by morning. In fact, when it was time to get up, she insisted that the sun hurt her eyes too much and asked that all the drapes in the house be closed. Because the family didn't keep a coffin around, she said she'd spend the day sleeping under her bed.

"You're being ridiculous, Amanda," her father said, growing irritable. "Now, get yourself dressed and go to school."

Wearing sunglasses to protect her eyes from what she now insisted was a blinding glare, Amanda did go to school. She hardly lifted her head off her desk all day, claiming to be tired due to acute anemia. She even refused to attend gym class because of the mirrors in the girls' locker room. At lunchtime she ran from the cafeteria, screaming that the garlic bread served with the day's spaghetti special was going to kill her. And after school she rejected her mother's home-baked cookies, requesting a pint of Type O blood for her afternoon snack.

That night Amanda's parents sat her down for a stern talk.

"Amanda, enough is enough," her father began. "We put up with you when you thought you had kidney failure, black lung disease, beriberi, and typhoid fever. But vampirism is going just too far."

"Honey, we want you to see a counselor," her mother said gently.

"We have the name of an excellent therapist who is an expert on hypochondria," her father added. "We think you'll like him."

"Just because someone's a hypochondriac doesn't mean she can't really get sick!" Amanda shouted. "And just because you don't believe in vampires doesn't mean they don't exist! Now, if you want to help me, find me a dog or a cat or some other animal so I can drink its blood."

"All right, that's it," her father said, rising to his feet. "You're going to see the therapist first thing tomorrow morning, no ifs, ands, or buts. But right now I want you to march upstairs and go straight to bed. And no more talk of vampires."

Amanda did go to bed, but she didn't go to sleep. Lying under her covers, staring up at the ceiling, all she could think about was the gnawing hunger she felt deep in her stomach and the overwhelming urge she had to taste warm, salty blood. The urge was growing stronger by the moment, consuming her entire being.

Finally, unable to resist it any longer, Amanda climbed out of bed, opened her window, and looked down at the lawn twelve feet below. Ignoring the night's chill, she awkwardly climbed up onto the sill, stood poised on the narrow ledge, then spread her arms as if to fly.

"I hear your call, master!" she cried to her unseen vampire king. "Tonight I fly into your waiting arms!"

And with that, Amanda stepped off the ledge and launched herself into space.

The ambulance arrived at the hospital emergency room fifteen minutes later. X-rays revealed that Amanda was suffering from a broken leg as well as an ankle sprain and numerous bruises caused by the fall from her second-story window. Her leg was set in a plaster cast, her ankle was wrapped in an Ace bandage, and she was sent home with strict instructions to stay in bed for the next week.

"Well, I hope you're happy, young lady," her father said scornfully as they drove home at four o'clock in the morning. "Now you've *really* got something to complain about."

"By the way, we heard from the Liebermans," her mother added. "Remember the young vampire you danced with? It turns out he was a sophomore from West High who'd crashed the Lieberman's party. That's why he didn't tell you his name."

"So, you see, Amanda, this whole vampire thing was all in your head," her father concluded. "Just like your weeklong heart attack in third grade and the time you were convinced you had watermelons growing in your stomach."

Amanda remained silent in the backseat of her parents' car. She felt like a fool. Gazing out the window into the early morning darkness, she wondered how she ever believed that a simple scratch had been a vampire's bite. It was all so ridiculous!

But then, what had scratched her during the blackout at the Liebermans' party? And why wasn't the scratch on her neck healing? In fact, now it was starting to throb and itch.

She glanced out the window and noticed a full moon overhead. Then she remembered that Mr. Lieberman had said he'd seen two werewolves at the party. There had been a full moon out that night, too. Could one of them have been real? And could it have scratched her when the lights were out? If so, that meant . . .

"Amanda? What's wrong, dear?" her mother asked, turning around. "You don't look well. Are you getting carsick?"

"*Arrrrooooo!*" Amanda howled, suddenly feeling the urge to eat raw human flesh.

"What now?" her parents asked simultaneously, not even bothering to look in the backseat at their deranged daughter.

If they had, they would have seen the first few coarse hairs sprouting from Amanda's arms.

Camp Doom

here are vampires, and then there are vampires. In the movies, vampires are usually easy to recognize. They're tall and powerful, with pale skin, slicked-back hair, red-rimmed eyes, and snakelike fangs. They live in dark, gloomy castles, wear capes, speak in odd eastern European accents, and go by the name of Count whatever.

In real life, vampires aren't always so easy to spot. They tend to look just like ordinary people. They dress like you or me, and their skin has the same healthy glow as everyone else's. Unlike the vampires in books and movies, they can walk around in broad daylight, their images reflect in mirrors, and they can't turn themselves into bats. You don't need to run a wooden stake through their hearts to kill them—a drop from a ten-story building will do just fine. Oh, and they don't suck blood, either.

By now, you're probably thinking, what is this kid

talking about? If these people don't even suck blood, how can they be vampires? Maybe I should start at the beginning.

My name is Glen Okita. I'm thirteen years old and I live on the East Side of Milwaukee, Wisconsin. I'm an A-minus student at Henry Crane Junior High School, where I'm also a star soccer player and a member of the Astronomy Club. I like sports, science, music, and action movies. I don't believe in ghosts or monsters or any of that supernatural stuff. Or, at least I didn't—until I met the vampire.

It was late June, and my folks had decided to send me to summer camp for four weeks. The place was called Camp Waupaca and was located up in Wisconsin's North Woods. It offered boating, fishing, sports, hiking, camping, and even go-carts. I'd never been away from home for more than a few nights at a time, but it sounded like a fun place. Besides, it sure beat staying at home and looking after my dumb eight-year-old sister while my parents went to work. So I agreed to give it a try.

After a five-hour drive through the heart of Wisconsin, we finally arrived at Camp Waupaca. The camp contained a dozen log cabins set on the eastern shore of a large lake in the midst of one of the most beautiful forests I'd ever seen.

The main building, called the Lodge, was two stories tall. It had a large recreation room featuring Ping-Pong, pinball, video games, and card tables, as well as the mess hall where we'd have most of our meals.

This was where we met the camp director, Mr. Whorley. He was a huge, jolly man with a big droopy mustache and only a fringe of rust red hair visible beneath his ever-present Brewers baseball cap. He gave us a tour of the place, including the lake, the boathouse, the tennis courts, the baseball field, and the go-cart track. Then, after my folks left, he dropped me off at my bunkhouse.

It was a small cabin the kids liked to call the "pig sty." There were eight bunks in all, and since I was one of the first campers to arrive, I got to pick the bed I wanted. I selected one of the lower bunks near a window and had just finished stowing my clothes in my footlocker when another kid entered the bunkhouse and introduced himself.

"Hi, I'm Ethan Douglas," he said, offering his hand. "I've got the upper bunk over there."

Ethan looked to be about my age and height and had a bright, warm smile and a head full of curly blond hair.

"I'm Glen Okita," I said, shaking his hand.

As soon as our palms touched, I felt a sharp, tingling sensation in my right arm. At the same time my legs became weak, as if the floor had suddenly dropped away beneath me. The feeling lasted only a second, and when it had passed, I found myself wondering if it had even happened at all.

"Ethan here is from Hawk River," Mr. Whorley said, suddenly appearing in the cabin's doorway. "Glen's from Milwaukee. I think you two should hit it off just fine."

"I'm sure we will," Ethan said, smiling. "In fact, I think we're going to be best friends."

By dinnertime, all my other bunkmates had shown up, and the pig sty was full. We were all twelve- and thirteen-year-olds. Some, like Ethan, were from small towns. Others, like me, were from big cities. One of the boys, Jerry Silver, had come all the way from Philadelphia.

At the mess hall we were assigned Table 6, and it was here that we met our counselor. Tom Vanderhayden was a big, muscular eighteen-year-old jock who was about to start his freshman year at the University of Wisconsin. "If any of you kids ever has any trouble, you come to me," Tom said. "I want us all to have a great summer. Okay?"

"Okay!" we all shouted in unison, then dug into our burgers, fries, and lemonade.

Dinner was followed by what Mr. Whorley called an orientation meeting, where the camp rules were outlined. Then we broke up into groups and spent the next two hours goofing off in the Lodge before getting ready for bed.

Lights-out was at ten o'clock sharp. I was afraid I was going to have trouble sleeping. I'd always had a hard time falling asleep in strange places, and out here in the country with all the weird cricket noises and the sounds of the other seven boys tossing and turning in their bunks, I was sure it was going to be a restless night.

But, surprisingly, as soon as I closed my eyes, I was out. And I slept solidly, without having so much as a single dream, until I felt a hand roughly shaking my shoulder.

"Let's go, Okita!" Tom Vanderhayden bellowed into my ear, still trying to shake me awake. "You going to sleep the whole day?"

"Huh?" I said groggily. I squinted into the bright sun already blasting through the nearby window. "What time is it?"

"Nine-thirty," Tom said. "You've slept all the way through breakfast!"

I couldn't believe it. How could I have not heard the other kids wake up and get dressed?

"Where is everyone?" I asked, my head still foggy with sleep.

"Over at the ball field picking teams," Tom replied. "You'd better hurry up and get over there if you don't want to be left out."

I bolted up in bed and felt the blood rush from my head. I felt weak. Not the tired, achy kind of weak that comes with the flu. No, this was a complete and total lack of energy. It was as if sometime during the night, someone had attached wires to my arms and literally sucked all the life force out of my body. In fact, I felt so weak that all I could do was sit there and stare blankly into space.

"Are you all right?" Tom asked, concerned.

"Yeah, yeah," I managed to say with effort. "I'm fine."

"Are you sick?" He bent down and took a closer look at my face.

"Just give me a minute," I insisted, somehow managing to swing my legs over the side of the bunk and get up.

It took me most of the morning to shower and get dressed. I joined the others for lunch and felt much better after I ate. By mid-afternoon I was out swimming in the lake with all the other "pigs," and the morning's strange events eventually seemed less and less important.

That night I again fell asleep at ten sharp, but this time I woke up at seven o'clock feeling refreshed and went to breakfast with the rest of the campers. It wasn't until we were halfway through our scrambled eggs and bacon that Matt Kinchloe, a kid from South Milwaukee, announced that Jerry Silver hadn't shown up for breakfast.

"Last time I saw him, he was still in bed," Greg Gonzalez, who was also from Milwaukee, offered.

"Maybe he's sick," some other guy whose name I didn't know yet suggested.

"I'll go see if I can find him," said Tom, rising from the table. "You all be sure to clean your plates, now."

After Tom left, I mentioned to my bunkmates how weak I'd felt the previous morning, but how the sensation had passed by mid-afternoon.

"Maybe it's some kind of virus," Matt said.

"Yeah," I agreed. "Maybe there's something going around."

Ethan Douglas, who'd been sitting at the end of the table eating in silence, looked down at his breakfast and smiled. He looked like a kid who knew a juicy little secret, one the other kids would kill to know. And as it turned out, that was exactly the case.

* * *

Whatever this "bug" was that had hit Camp Waupaca, it continued to play havoc with us kids in the pig sty. Every day one of us would sleep abnormally late and finally wake up feeling weak and depressed. The feeling would last for three hours or so, then go away after we had managed to force down our noon meal.

Most of us continued to explain it away as some kind of twenty-four-hour virus. But after two weeks or more of watching this pattern unfold, Matt Kinchloe and I became suspicious.

"Have you noticed that one of us is sick every morning?" Matt said as we all set off on a five-mile-long hike around the lake. "And it's not just that somebody's always sick, it's that it's always just one person. Not two. Not three. Just one."

"I know," I said. "And no one else in camp seems to be getting sick. It's just us kids in the pig sty."

"Not *all*," Matt pointed out, his voice containing a dark edge. "That blond kid, Ethan . . . he's never been sick once."

Matt was right. By this time most of us, Matt and me included, had been hit with the alleged bug twice. But Ethan had remained mysteriously immune.

"So what are you saying?" I asked Matt uneasily. "That Ethan's the one who's *making* us sick?"

"I don't know," Matt said, his eyes fixed on Ethan, who was walking about twenty feet ahead of us. "There's just something about the guy that gives me the creeps."

Suddenly, as if he had heard us, Ethan turned and glanced back our way. Catching my eye, he smiled. He was wearing that same creepy I-know-something-you-don't-know grin, only this time it was directed straight at me. I didn't like it. I didn't like it one bit.

The very next morning, tragedy struck.

There had been no hint of danger in the air. The sky was clear. The sun was warm. There was a light, warm breeze blowing from the west. We had assembled at the lake as usual at ten o'clock and set out on the water in canoes, two to a boat. I was with Jerry Silver.

We were out only about ten minutes when both of us heard screaming nearby. We turned to see that Ethan's canoe had capsized. Ethan himself was in the water, yelling for help while, at the same time struggling to stay afloat. His partner, Matt Kinchloe, was nowhere to be seen.

Tom Vanderhayden and his partner, Greg Gonzalez, were the first on the scene. Tom dived into the water and helped Ethan upright his overturned canoe and climb aboard. He then dived beneath the surface and searched for Matt. He emerged several minutes later with the boy's limp body. I jumped into the water to help, and together Tom and I got Matt into Tom's canoe. Already his body felt cold and lifeless, and by the time we reached shore, there was no doubt about it: Matt was dead.

An ambulance was called and they took Matt's body to the nearest hospital for an autopsy. While we all waited for the results of the tests to come back, we asked Ethan to explain what had happened out on the lake.

"I don't know," Ethan insisted. "We were paddling along when, all of a sudden, Matt just keeled over. When I leaned forward to see what was wrong, the canoe capsized. The next thing I knew, I was in the water."

"Maybe it's the bug," Jerry Silver offered. "You know how it knocks us out."

"But when we get sick, it's always first thing in the morning," I countered. "It would have worn off by the time we went canoeing."

No one else said a word.

We didn't get the autopsy report till the next day. Mr. Whorley called us all together so we'd know the facts and not spread crazy rumors. According to the doctors, Matt hadn't drowned. In fact, he'd been dead before he even hit the water. The official conclusion was that Matt had suffered a massive heart attack.

"It's rare, but it happens, I guess," Mr. Whorley said, clearly not comfortable with the verdict himself.

After the meeting, I asked Mr. Whorley for more specifics about the autopsy report. I explained that my father was a doctor and that the report he gave us seemed incomplete.

"Do you know if Matt had a history of heart disease?" I asked.

"There's no mention of it in his camp medical records," Mr. Whorley admitted.

"What about in the autopsy report?" I pressed on. "Did it say anything about any evidence of heart disease?"

"No, as a matter of fact, it didn't," Mr. Whorley said, obviously troubled himself. "All they know is, Matt's heart just . . . stopped."

*   *   *

I had trouble sleeping that night. I'd drift off, only to be awakened by visions of poor Matt Kinchloe's body being pulled from the water. I remembered how cold his body felt, and I shivered. Being immersed in lake water for less than five minutes, there's no reason Matt's body should have felt so positively *lifeless*. It was as if all the life force had been drained out of him by some sort of energy pump.

I turned over, trying to get comfortable, and briefly opened my eyes. At first I wasn't quite sure what I was seeing. But then, as my eyes grew accustomed to the gloom, the picture grew frighteningly clear. Someone was kneeling over Jerry Silver's bunk. He had his fingers outstretched and placed on either side of Jerry's upturned face. As I watched in growing dread, I heard Jerry's breathing become labored as if he was fighting for his life.

Alarmed, I leaned forward, trying to determine if what I thought I was seeing was true. I must have made a noise, for the figure bending over Jerry turned and looked straight at me. It was Ethan Douglas.

Ethan immediately released Jerry, who fell back onto his pillow like a rag doll. He then raced across the room and slapped a hand over my mouth before I could shout a warning. Just as it had when we first shook hands two weeks earlier, the touch of his skin on mine created a mild electric shock that left me momentarily stunned.

"Shhhh!" Ethan said softly, his eyes burning red in the darkness. "Jerry's going to be fine. And so will you . . . as long as you keep quiet."

He carefully removed his hand from my mouth. I barely knew how to respond.

"You—you *killed* Matt Kinchloe," I found myself sputtering.

"There's no way to prove that," Ethan said matter-of-factly. "Modern medical science doesn't admit the existence of 'people' like me."

"Just what *are* you?" I asked, my mind still a jumble of questions.

"I'm just like you—only different," Ethan grinned evilly. "Better, in fact. You see, many thousands of years ago my people learned the secret to good health and long life. We developed the ability to literally absorb life's essence from other creatures—other people—so we could survive."

"You mean, you've been *feeding* off us?" I gasped, realizing that this thing I was speaking to was not a boy at all, but some kind of vampire.

"I took nothing you'd miss," Ethan said. "What essence I 'borrowed,' you regained within hours."

"But Matt Kinchloe—" I stammered.

"He figured out what I am," Ethan explained, "and he was going to expose me. I had no choice but to drain him—completely. Even your laws recognize the need for self-preservation."

I shuddered, contemplating the fate that surely lay before me. A fate exactly like poor Matt Kinchloe's.

"Wait!" I said, struggling to keep my voice low. "If I die like Matt did, that would be too much of a coincidence. There'll be questions. People will know it's murder."

"I know," Ethan said, "which is why I'm going to keep you alive . . . for now. Keep your mouth shut and maybe you'll stay that way a long time."

"And you expect me to forget what I just saw?" I asked, referring to what Ethan had just done to Jerry.

114

"Just a bad dream," Ethan said flatly. And with that, he touched his index finger to my forehead and I was out like a light.

* * *

The remainder of my four weeks at Camp Waupaca passed without serious incident. I sailed. I fished. I played ball. I made some crafts. I should have enjoyed myself, but I didn't. I was living under a cloud, surviving from day to day at the whim of a boy who could kill me at any moment with nothing but his touch.

When the month was over and I returned home to Milwaukee, I still lived in fear. Ethan had referred to "his people," which meant that he was not alone. They could be anywhere—at school, at the mall, at the baseball stadium. Unlike the bloodsuckers of Hollywood, these real-life vampires look no different from us and probably walk among us every day.

So let this be fair warning. If you value your life's essence, stay alert. And be very, very careful about who you touch.

Roadkill

Jess Tanner's family had been on the highway for nearly twelve straight hours. They had stopped only twice to gas the car, to restock their food supplies, and of course, to use the bathroom. Otherwise, Jess's father had been driving "pedal to the metal," as he liked to say, screaming down Interstate 50 like people with a long way to go and no time to get there.

The Tanner family always spent their summer vacations burning up America's highways. The family set out in a four-door sedan crammed with economy-sized bags of salty snack foods, half-folded highway maps, travel-sized board games, and plastic bags brimming with warm, overripe fruit. No matter where Jess's parents decided the family would vacation—a national park, a resort, a big city, the beach, the mountains, or the desert—they always drove. Even if their destination was clear across the country, traveling by any means other than the family car was out of the question, at least as far as Jess's father was concerned.

"Flying's too expensive," Mr. Tanner always said. "And trains confine you to *their* schedules. When you drive, *you're* in control."

Jess would point out the cost of gas, hotels, meals, and other travel expenses, somehow hoping to get his father to spring for plane tickets. Then he'd talk about being able to relax and let someone else do the driving, hoping to make his dad reconsider going by train or plane. But his dad always had an answer for every argument, an answer that put them right back on the highway, trapped in a shiny metal box with wheels.

"When you drive," Mr. Tanner insisted, "you get to see America!"

This was true, Jess had to agree. When you flew, you were usually at your destination in just a few hours. All you got to see along the way were broad, endless landscapes and the fairytale-like cloud kingdoms that existed at thirty thousand feet. When you took the train, you only had a chance to sit in plush, glass-topped observation cars and roam freely up and down the aisles. But when you drove, you spent days and days belted into a cramped seat looking at endless cornfields or acres of swamp or miles of desert. Usually the agonizing boredom would be broken only by the sight of an occasional billboard, freight train, or grain elevator.

Of course, when things *really* got boring, you could always turn on the farmer's markets radio and listen to the local reports. You might even be lucky enough to pick up a country/western station that would waver in and out for about five minutes before completely disappearing into a hail of hissing static.

Jess Tanner *hated* these yearly car trips. He hated sharing the backseat with his younger sister, Grace, and he hated how she'd always poke him in the side when he wasn't looking, then quickly turn away and deny she'd ever touched him. He hated fishing warm soda cans out of the water-filled bottoms of coolers that never really kept anything cold. And perhaps most of all, he hated how his father never, *ever* made motel reservations in advance. Mr. Tanner stopped to sleep only when he got tired. Which was almost never.

"Come on, guys, one more exit!" Mr. Tanner would inevitably say whenever the rest of the family pleaded with him to pull off the interstate and look for a place to spend the night. "It's still early. Let's put a few more miles behind us! You'll be grateful tomorrow that we drove a few extra miles tonight."

Today this "one more exit" speech had begun around 7:30 P.M. It had been repeated six times as they sped by a half dozen perfectly respectable restaurant/motel complexes. It was now nearly 9:00, and Jess was becoming desperate. He wanted to eat real food. He wanted to sleep in a real bed. And most of all, he just wanted to stand up and stretch his legs before they became permanently bent.

"Come on, Dad, let's pull off," he whined. "I'm tired. I want to have dinner. Look!" He pointed at a highway sign that showed that an exit with several motels and restaurants was only five miles ahead. "We can pull off there and stay the night."

"Just one more exit," his father insisted. "We're making great time. Why kill the momentum?"

Jess flopped back into his seat and sighed in frustration. He felt a sharp poke in his right side, then spun around in time to see his sister turn away and innocently look out her window.

"Stop it, Grace!" Jess yelled.

"Huh? Stop what?" Grace asked unconvincingly.

"Both of you, just cut it out!" their mother said sharply. "We'll pull off in just a few more minutes. Now, sit back and relax."

Five minutes later the exit, with its brightly lit motels and beckoning burger joints, chicken emporiums, taco stands, and pizza parlors, flashed by in a colorful blur. Jess turned and sadly looked out the back window. The small oasis of civilization glowed momentarily like a beacon of hope in the endless darkness, then slowly faded into the night's gloom.

A few minutes later another highway sign appeared. This one read, "Next Exit—23 Miles."

"Twenty-three miles!" Jess groaned. "By then, I'll have starved to death! There will be nothing back here but two skeletons!"

"Oh, stop complaining," his father snapped. "We're on vacation. We're supposed to be having fun!"

"Will you promise to stop at the next exit?" Jess asked. "*Please.*"

"We'll see what's there," Mr. Tanner replied. "If it doesn't look promising, we'll keep going."

"No!" Jess protested. "We have to stop. You have to promise."

"It is getting rather late," Jess's mom agreed.

"And you did say you wanted to get an early start in the morning."

"All right, Jess," his father said, sounding somewhat disappointed. "We'll stop at the next exit."

"Promise?" Jess demanded.

"Promise," Mr. Tanner agreed.

Twenty minutes later the Tanners pulled off at Exit 116. At the bottom of the off-ramp they found only a two-lane road stretching off in either direction.

"There's nothing here," Mr. Tanner said flatly. "Let's try the next exit."

"No!" Jess yelled. "There has to be a place to stay around here somewhere. Maybe there's a town nearby."

"I think I see a faint glow off to the right," his mom said, coming to the rescue. "Maybe there's a town over there."

"All right," Mr. Tanner said reluctantly. "We'll check it out." He eased the car onto the two-lane road and headed toward the distant glow. "But if we don't find anything in five minutes, I'm turning around and getting back on the highway. I don't want us to get lost on some back road."

As luck would have it, it was exactly five minutes later when a small sign reading "Welcome to Schreckville" was illuminated briefly by the Tanners' headlights.

"Schreckville. What kind of a weird name is that?" Grace asked, grimacing.

"Probably named after its founder," Mr. Tanner explained. "You know, Mr. Ville."

The family's response to Mr. Tanner's bad joke was a deadly silence. Everyone was exhausted, stiff, and starving, and no one was in the mood to laugh—even if the joke had been funny. Finally Mrs. Tanner, the family's unofficial navigator, spoke up, her head buried in a road map.

"This is strange," she said. "Schreckville isn't on our map, and it's not listed in the travel guide."

But before anyone could respond, Grace shouted and pointed excitedly out the window. "Look! A restaurant!"

Indeed, they could now see a small roadside diner about five hundred feet ahead. The restaurant looked simple but fairly modern and had about a dozen cars in its parking lot.

"It looks busy, even this late at night," Mr. Tanner commented. "It must be very good."

"I don't care what they serve!" Jess said with more than a hint of desperation. "Let's eat!"

"All right, we'll stop here for dinner," said Mr. Tanner, flipping on his turn signal. "And while we're here, I'll find out if there are any good motels in the area."

Jess breathed a sigh of relief. They were finally stopping for the night. He turned his eyes heavenward and gave a silent prayer of thanks.

Mr. Tanner found a parking space and killed the engine. Then the family painfully eased themselves out of their seats, moaning and groaning as their rigid muscles were exercised for the first time in hours.

Hobbling on legs that felt like rubber bands, Jess headed for the restaurant. As he got closer, he noticed a sign in the window reading "The Bloody Good Cafe—All Types Served."

"That's an odd name for a restaurant," Grace commented, noticing the sign.

"It means the food is served raw," Jess responded with a dark, spooky tone designed to scare his little sister.

"It's probably meant to be like an old English pub," Mr. Tanner speculated. "The English use that expression a lot."

"Wonderful!" Mrs. Tanner said, delighted. "I love Yorkshire pudding."

"But what do they mean, 'All types served'?" Grace asked, still a little uneasy.

"It means they welcome all types of people," Mr. Tanner said confidently. "Even tired tourists like us. Now, come on, everyone. It's the Bloody Good Cafe or bust!"

They entered through the cafe's front door. Jess immediately noticed that the lighting was unusually dim for a roadside diner. In fact, the only light came from the glowing candles set on each table.

"My, how romantic!" Mrs. Tanner commented, clearly delighted.

They were immediately approached by a thin, pale, dark-haired woman about twenty years old. Her large, deep-set eyes scanned them critically, as if she was deciding whether or not to serve them.

"Table for four?" she finally asked, her voice containing a subtle note of disapproval.

"Please," Mr. Tanner replied. "We're starved!"

"Right this way," the young hostess said wearily. She led them to a square table along the far wall. "Your waiter will be right with you."

Moments after the hostess departed, Mrs. Tanner noticed that something was amiss. "She didn't give us any menus," she observed, looking about.

"Maybe the selections are on a blackboard somewhere," Jess suggested. It was then he noticed that everyone in the restaurant—about thirty or so people, all adults—were eyeing him and his family. It wasn't like they were outright staring, but every once in a while they'd throw a subtle glance at the Tanners, giving off signals of disapproval and even hostility.

Jess noticed two other odd things: all the other customers had the same pale, sunken-eyed look of the young hostess, and none of them were actually eating. Instead, all of them were drinking what looked like tomato juice.

He was about to comment on this when a pale young waiter with even darker, deeper-set eyes than their hostess's stepped up to the table.

"Hello, I'm Dimitri and I'll be your waiter this evening," the young man droned. "What type would you prefer tonight?"

"Type?" Mr. Tanner asked, obviously confused.

"Our special tonight is a wonderful German Type B blood pudding, unfiltered, warmed to ninety-eight point six degrees and served with a garnish of curdled lymphocytes," Dimitri recited from memory. "We also have an excellent French A-negative imported directly from the city of Bordeaux, and for those who prefer a little spice in their diet, we have a Chinese Szechuan Type O served over sweet-and-sour platelets."

Jess was feeling sick to his stomach. He wasn't quite sure what Dimitri was talking about, but whatever it was, he knew it had something to do with blood. And this restaurant and its customers were very, very weird.

From the look of things, the rest of his family was having the same uncomfortable reaction. Mr. Tanner, ever the optimist, struggled to maintain his usual jovial mood.

"That all sounds . . . er . . . delicious," Mr. Tanner said, forcing a smile. "But I think we'd all prefer something . . . well . . . a bit more simple. You know, like a hamburger."

The entire room suddenly fell silent. Jess looked around. Now everyone in the place definitely *was* looking at them. He could see drops of thick tomato juice dripping from a number of their sneering mouths. Or was it tomato juice?

"A *hamburger*?" Dimitri said, his voice dripping with disgust. "You came to this cafe for cooked meat? What kind of vampires are you?"

"Vampires?" Mr. Tanner asked, obviously confused. "Is this some kind of a joke?"

Jess reached over and grabbed his father's arm. "Dad, I think maybe we'd better be going," he said softly.

"They're not one of us," an older man said from across the room.

"They're mortals!" gasped a thin, blond-haired woman seated at another table.

"Fresh blood!" chortled a young man, baring what to Jess looked like a wickedly sharp pair of canine teeth.

"No!" said the young man's dinner companion, a woman with short red hair. "We are civilized. We must behave according to the New Order."

"The New Order can rot in a shallow grave!" the young man bellowed. "I'm six hundred years old, and I can make my own decisions!"

He knocked his blood red drink aside with one swipe of his hand, then stood and faced the stunned Tanners.

"Welcome, honored guests, to Schreckville," the young man said, making a dramatic bow. "It appears you've come a long way. Please stay the night. We'd *love* to have you for dinner!"

The young vampire's full-grown fangs glistened menancingly in the candlelight. He was about to launch himself at Mr. Tanner's neck when three of the other patrons grabbed him and struggled to hold him back.

"No, Gregor! You must control The Hunger!" one of the other customers insisted. "If we kill live prey, the humans will hunt us down like they did in the old days. They will kill us. They will run stakes through us all. Please don't do this!"

Jess turned to his father, who was just sitting there struck dumb with shock, and whispered, "Uh, Dad? I think it's time to go . . . *now!*"

"Good idea," Mr. Tanner said woodenly. As if by reflex, he slapped a few dollars onto the table, then hustled his family to the door. "Sorry, everyone. Gotta get an early start in the morning."

They stumbled out of the restaurant and raced back to their car. They were heading back down the two-lane highway toward Interstate 50 before Jess realized that he still had his dinner napkin stuffed into the front of his shirt.

"Mom, what was that all about?" Grace finally spoke up. "Why were all those strange people looking at us?"

"Quiet, dear," Mrs. Tanner said, trying her best to control the terror that was still gripping her body. "Let your father drive."

The Tanners drove on in tense silence. No one dared say what they were all thinking: that they had just stumbled into a colony of modern-day vampires and had barely escaped with their lives. It was as if speaking the words out loud would make the experience that much more real. Yes, it was better to stay silent, to quietly convince themselves, each in his or her own way, that what had happened was only a fantasy or a bad dream.

Reaching the interstate, Mr. Tanner spun onto the on-ramp. He quickly merged with the smattering of westbound traffic and set his cruise control for sixty miles per hour.

Finally back in familiar surroundings, the Tanners began to breathe again. Mrs. Tanner looked at her road map, her hands clutching it so tightly that her fingers were beet red.

"There's another exit coming up in a few minutes," she reported, a slight tremor in her voice. "The guide says there are several motels and restaurants right off the highway there."

Just then, there was a loud *thump* on the roof of their car. Jess jumped in his seat. In his mind, he imagined that the young vampire from the cafe had somehow escaped and had followed them all this way. He imagined that the creature had just landed on the roof of their car and was ready to suck the blood from their living bodies to satisfy its ancient appetite.

His heart pounding in his chest, Jess leaned forward and spoke softly to his father. "We're not tired. Let's drive all the way till dawn."

Mr. Tanner just nodded his head and pointed the car into the endless night.